I0535515

THE DISPLACED

vol. 1
the corpocracy series

BOB D'EITH

ADAGIO BOOKS

VANCOUVER, BC

Written by Bob D'Eith

Copyright © 2014 Adagio Books (div. of Adagio Music Inc.)

All rights reserved. This book or any portion thereof may not be reproduced or used in any manner whatsoever without the express written permission of the publisher except for the use of brief quotations in a book review.

The characters and events in this book are fictitious. Any similarity to real persons, living or dead, is coincidental and not intended by the author.

Printed in the United States of America

First Printing, 2014

ISBN 978-0-9919930-1-7

Adagio Books (div. Adagio Music Inc.)
100-938 Howe Street
Vancouver, B.C.
Canada
V6Z 1N9

www.adagiomusic.ca

Acknowledgements:

To my amazing wife Kim and my children Sheldon, Braden, Amy, Cameron, and Aryn. You get me up every morning, literally and figuratively. I love you all.

Braden D'Eith, thanks for your help with the graphic design. You probably saved me ten hours of head scratching.

Special thanks to my editor, Wren Handman, for challenging me to be a better writer and for her impeccable eye for detail.

THE DISPLACED

PART I Down Below

The Joint Stock Companies Act of 1856 in the UK was the beginning of the modern company. The basic principal was that the corporate structure limited liability for shareholders, protecting them from personal lawsuits. This made investment more palatable, allowing risky overseas trade to flourish. Companies became legal "persons" who dominated the entire global economy. The purpose of a company was to make profit for its shareholders; it had no heart and no soul. In fact, if a board of directors acted benevolently towards society, leading to a loss in profit, the shareholders would be well within their rights to sue the directors. The government's role in all of this was to act as the conscience for the company. Regulation was meant to ensure that the quest for profit was tempered by the needs of the community. If, however, a government was usurped by corporate interests, leading to complete deregulation, then a Corporatocracy (or Corpocracy as it would be commonly referred to) would ensue, a system of governing that would put the pursuit of profit *ahead of everything else. - **Cassandra Taylor, chief colonial historian***

Chapter 1

Matt sat on his garage-sale couch contemplating how he got here, a roach infested rental just outside the spaceport complex in New Dallas. At least he had his holoscreen and his old school 2-D movies. *They don't make them like they used to.* He had spent the last ten years trying to right a wrong that had happened to his family, but that was ancient history now. Nobody cared about the Displaced any more. When 911-2 happened on September 11, 2053, the suitcase nukes had destroyed entire city centers. Matt's family was lucky to survive, having gone camping on the Oregon coast that horrifying week. The family had lost everything when Seattle was destroyed – friends, family, their very home. Dallas and Toronto were hit at the same time, on the same day. Other bombs failed or were thwarted in Washington, New York, and Los Angeles. It came out of nowhere, when most people had forgotten about the old Gulf Wars and the War on Terror. Perhaps someone should have listened when the pundits of the time warned that relentless bombing of civilians would lead to generations of new fundamentalists and terrorists. The world had once again been on the brink of all-out nuclear war, but massive retaliatory strikes by the USA, Canada, and the UK on terrorist targets around the globe were authorized by the international community. A huge pressure valve was released. When the dust settled, it was clear that the world would never be the same again, just like after the first 911.

Matt Taylor's family had become one of the Displaced. With no home they were put into camps by the government. Many of the Displaced were sick from radiation poisoning. For a period, international relief agencies helped them to survive. Even though millions of dollars were raised through massive virtu-concerts, most of that money ended up in everyone's hands other than the Displaced. In the end, hundreds of thousands of people were left to fend for themselves. It was just too big a problem.

At the New Republican debates of 2055, delegates cheered when Presidential candidates spoke of the great American tradition of the survival of the fittest: *just let the Displaced fend for themselves.* That attitude had lit a fire in Matt's belly. He saw tens of thousands of people go from happy citizens to impoverished outcasts. Of those who survived, many chose to become laborers for the massive New Dallas facility, doing dangerous work for a pittance in wages. Others tried to re-integrate into other cities, but found a lot of shut doors and scarce jobs after the Great Market Crash that followed 911-2.

Jonas Harris, Matt's best friend from childhood, was not one of the Displaced. His family had moved to Sunset Hill in upscale Seattle when they were in the eleventh grade. Jonas' dad had made millions launching a super-app for buying groceries. The area where the bombs went off, where Matt's family had lived, would be unlivable for many years, but Sunset Hill survived without a blemish. They were lucky that the winds were blowing from the north that day instead of from the south; just dumb luck. Jonas went to the best schools and waltzed his way into a great job overlooking the very slum where the Displaced worked, eking out their menial existence. Matt looked up at the Spaceport tower lights and his blood boiled. Where was the justice for *his* people.

Matt had worked in the spaceport as a mechanic with his dad for years. He was lucky to have a job. The family had moved when it was apparent that there were no jobs in the Pacific North-West. Matt had done his very best to organize and lobby, but with trade unions having been basically outlawed during the Second Reagan years, everything had to be done under the table. It got really tough when his dad had died along with a lot of other buddies in the Moon mining colony construction yard fire of 2057. After that, his mom had gone to stay with her aging parents in Portland. He had been alone for nearly five years now in New Dallas.

Matt put his head in his hands. *Maybe it's time to give up*, he thought. *I'm so stupid thinking I could actually do anything.* He got up and walked to the fridge. Matt chuckled to himself. *At least we can still get beer.* Just as he was twisting off the top of his lager with calloused hands, his eyephone blinked. *Who the heck would be calling at this hour?* He tapped his implant and a ghost image appeared of his old pal Jonas. *Jesus, what does* he *want.*

"Hey buddy! Long time, no see. How's things in the burbs?" Matt looked around him and shook his head ever so slightly, gritting his teeth. Jonas was Matt's physical opposite in many ways. Jonas was slightly above average in height and had close-cropped dirty blonde hair and startling blues eyes. Matt, on the other hand, was six-foot-three, with shaggy long brown hair, brown eyes, and a tough looking face. Jonas was a pretty boy; Matt was what women might call ruggedly handsome.

"Still a grease monkey. Getting those ships ready to take your beautiful, well-fed assholes for a trip they'll never forget. Funny, they never talk about space sickness in the brochures."

"Still got that old chip, hey buddy? Listen, I need a favor. Can I come by tonight and have a little chat in person?" Jonas looked around as if to make sure no one was listening.

"If you bring the beer, you can come, but I have an early shift, so I can't stay up late." He was puzzled, but could use the company. "And bring some bug spray, the roaches are getting bigger every day." Matt flashed Jonas his geo.

Now Jonas' car would remember where he lived; he doubted Jonas did.

Matt looked around at his dump of a pad. He thought about tidying up a bit, but decided, *Fuck it, I don't give a shit what Jonas thinks.* With that he slumped down on the couch with a big sigh, put his feet up on the chipped coffee table, turned on his holoscreen, and took a good pull from his bottle.

…murders in New Dallas, making it the murder capitol of the USA for the second straight year.

Twenty-eight year old Pop star New Messiah set herself on fire on the popular late night show After Dark Live. A spokesman from Extremely Loud Records stated that New Messiah will be missed by her millions of fans. He went on to say that in dying so young she will be immortalized in the same way as Marilyn Monroe and Princess Diana. Sales of New Messiah merchandise immediately spiked.

In other news, ultra-right-wing New Republican candidate Buddy Jones has taken the lead in the race for the Presidential candidacy. Incumbent Democratic President Lyndon James was not available for comment.

Matt drained the rest of his beer. *Just another day in paradise.*

Chapter 2

Jonas was fidgeting in the car. He surfed through some vid feeds, jonesing for days gone by when he could actually have driven his car. The institution of an automatic traffic grid had effectively neutered his ride. He just wanted to let off some steam and floor it, but instead he had to sit and try to amuse himself, which was difficult with what he had just overheard. He could barely stop himself from screaming. *Why did I have to hear that? I have an awesome life with everything I ever wanted.*

Jonas took a deep breath. *Matt will know what to do. He's practical. He lives and works in the trenches. He's dealt with this crap before.*

Finally, the car arrived at the destination. *What a shit hole.* Jonas looked up at the cheaply built apartments. They looked like they would fall down at the first gust of wind. *How can anyone live here?*

The front door was open and the buzzers were all smashed, and as he headed in he saw graffiti all over the interior walls. He made his way up the three flights of stairs to Matt's apartment. *Of course the elevator is broken.* 301. He knocked on the door. He heard a muffled voice, a bunch of locks unlatching, and then Matt opened the door. Jonas took a look at his old friend. Bushy, unkempt brown hair, broken nose, tired eyes. *He looks a hundred years old, man, poor dude.*

Jonas flashed his perfect set of teeth, and Matt swore he actually saw a twinkle. Coifed hair, trendy clothes, the latest bling. *Jesus, this guy really pisses me off.* But, Matt cracked a crooked smile and gave his old friend a big bear hug. He just couldn't hate his old pal; they had way too much history.

Jonas pushed by quickly and immediately started pacing. Matt saw that he was clearly agitated. "Jonas, chill man. What's going on?"

"Maybe, a drink, buddy?"

"I thought you were bringing the booze?"

"Crap, left it in the car."

"Right, heard that one before." Matt pulled a couple of cold ones out of the fridge. He gave one to Jonas, and chugged his own down.

"Okay, so we need to talk. I mean, I need to tell you something. I mean, I heard something that I shouldn't have heard." Jonas was starting to sweat.

"Slow down. Come sit, man, and take a breath. You're freaking me out."

"Yeah, sorry." Jonas sat down and slowed his breathing a bit. He went on, "Okay. So, I was working late and had to go to the can. I was in the stall, totally minding my own business, when our CEO came in with someone else. I recognized the CEO's voice, but not the other guy. Anyway, Mr. Kerr, the CEO, started talking about the new colonial flights. He said that there was a problem with the new hibernation units. They expected a pretty high failure rate. The other guy laughed and said something like 'Who cares, they'll be millions of miles away before anyone notices. Just do your job and shut the fuck up.'"

Jonas looked squarely at Matt. "What the hell am I supposed to do?"

Matt sat there for a second. The saddest thing was that he wasn't shocked at all by what Jonas was saying. He worked at the spaceport, and there was a lot of cost cutting going on. Big multinational companies were making billions of dollars on the colonization program. Problem was, a lot of *his* people were going up in those ships. There were long waiting lists. Waiting for what? A chance to die millions of miles away from home?

"Listen, Jonas. You have to be smart about this. These people will not hesitate to ice you if you're a troublemaker. People die every day on the port sites. I think you should go back to work and pretend that nothing happened. Leave this with me. If you hear anything else, be more careful next time. Don't come running here. We'll figure out some kind of way to communicate without being traced, okay?"

Jonas was visibly calmer now. His buddy had come through as he always did. "Thanks. You're right. No point overreacting."

Jonas got up, gave Matt a big hug, and made for the door.

Chapter 3

Mr. Kerr looked out the window of his hundredth floor penthouse office. While he had gotten over the vertigo from the view months ago, he still marveled at the vista; he could see for hundreds of miles. He had truly made it. Thirty years of clawing his way up the corporate ladder and now he ran Worldstar, the second largest space company in the world. Mr. Kerr was well aware that his success came with a price. Some would have called them the Illuminati as in some novels, but Mr. Kerr knew that there was nothing enlightened about them. The fact was that the real world order had become a true Corpocracy. Yes, there were still governments running the highways and schools and issuing licenses, but all around the world the big decisions, like wars, money, elections, were all controlled by an elite few. The public knew this in their hearts, but throughout the world there seemed to be a willful blindness. As long as families were housed, fed, and entertained, there weren't a lot of complaints. Mr. Kerr knew better. Companies were created for the sole purpose of making profit for their owners. They had no soul. No conscience. Unregulated, they always made decisions based on the bottom line. How many times had Mr. Kerr heard "acceptable human losses" when the bean counters showed the board of directors charts and graphs detailing risk of litigation vs. profit margin? No consideration was made to the people these decisions affected. Mr. Kerr was part of that machine, and that machine was part of a bigger machine. And that bigger machine was controlled by a small number of unelected, super rich people. Really, after all of the progress that humankind had made over the millennia, they were back to a feudal state. Only now kings, nobles, and peasants were called Super Elites, CEOs, and everyone else. The Kingdom of Company.

Worldstar did shuttle thousands of people a year up to the orbiting space hotels so that they could "ooh and ahh" at the happy blue planet; however the true purpose of Worldstar was to secure space supremacy for the Company.

Mr. Kerr sighed and turned back to his desk. He touched the implant on his temple and his desk lit up with holoreports, daily news feeds, market analyses, and of course a continuous reel of his latest big fishing adventure.

The hibernation unit problem was filed away along with hundreds of other little cost/benefit issues. Already forgotten, Mr. Kerr got back to work.

Chapter 4

Matt's shift came way too early. He hadn't slept well knowing that some of his people were at risk. *Poor Jonas. He's a good guy, just shallow. He's gonna have a hard time moving up in that nasty world.*

He shook the cobwebs out of his brain and grabbed a quick protein pack. He made it to the commuter train just as the doors were closing. The train was packed, and smelled of BO and oil. *Nice. I love my life.*

When Matt got to his station, he got his work orders for the day. Looking at the dirty screen he saw that his quota had gone up again. He did some quick math in his head - he would have to work a double to get everything done. Matt messaged his super to ask what was up, but instead of a personal response, a general holo came though his eyephone. That name still cracked him up. Apple had gone ballistic back in the day when people started calling their "Ocular Holoprojector Implants" eyephones. But the name stuck, and Apple managed to get a big settlement.

The image of Matt's yard boss came up. "Ok, folks, time to roll up those sleeves. We have a deadline to meet and we're behind on our deliverables. Sorry, only regular hour pay for this one. No overtime. Don't shoot the messenger. Right, back to work you grease monkeys."

No overtime. It just gets better and better. How do they get away with it? Oh yeah, we have no rights. Matt gathered his tools and made off for the ship compartment that he was working on. Installing zero-g sinks today. *Yippeekayay.*

As he walked to Supply, Matt tried to figure out how he could get to the hibernation guys. The massive vessels were mainly built in the orbiting shipyards, but many of the onboard electronics and hibernation components were built on Earth, right in New Dallas, then ferried up to the yards. There was one guy he knew from the watering hole that worked in that unit. *What was his name? Jones or James. Jamie, that was it.*

Tapping his implant, Matt called up a directory of workers. *Freakin' hopeless. Always out of date. Nobody cares about this stuff.* He went to his hololist and, seemingly poking the air, he chose Sandy. *She'll know, brainiac.*

Sandy's image came up right away. She was obviously working hard on some project. Matt thought the oil smudged on her cheek was kinda cute. "Hey, Matt, busy right now. Crazy quota today. What's up?"

"Nothing really, just trying to track down that guy Jamie. You know, that guy up in HLP?" The Human Life Preservation unit worked on hiberchamber technology for the sleeper ships.

"That jerk. Yeah, I know him." Matt suddenly remembered that Sandy and Jamie had a thing once. Maybe that was why he had thought of her. *Oops.*

"Just need a contact for him, that's all."

"I'll send it now. Tell him he's an asshole for me." She logged out and Matt got a contact flash. Matt had to think how to play this without raising any suspicion. He liked to think while he walked. It somehow gave him focus. *Okay, Jamie works in HLP and I'm installing sinks. No connection there. I could ask him if he wants to meet up for lunch. No, that would be weird. How about Tom's birthday this weekend? Maybe I could put something together for that. Get a bunch of guys to a party.* Tom was a good guy who worked in the same department as Matt. They had been drinking buddies for a long time.

Matt flashed Jamie about a party for Tom at the Ship on Friday. He then flashed a bunch of other guys. *Plant the seed.*

Matt's day was busy but uneventful, and the work gave him a lot of time to think. *Building another bloody starship.* Hypersonic travel was the new craze: horizontal take-off and landing, with just enough juice to hook up with the orbiting hotels and space stations in low-orbit, and get around the world in just hours. It was actually what should have been done originally, instead of the early space race and shuttle programs. Focusing only on the development of rocket technology really set space exploration back decades. The smarter thing would have been to have developed hypersonic travel, built space stations, and launched to the moon and beyond from space. Why deal with the atmosphere if you didn't have to? Politics and bureaucracy. That was what held humans back getting into space.

Ironically, it was private enterprise that reinvigorated space travel. Pioneers like Sir Richard Branson's Virgin Galactic paved the way for private ownership of space exploration. Of course, once the Company became solidified, all of the entrepreneurial companies were swallowed up. It was the nature of the beast. And that beast was voracious.

Matt got a ping. Jamie was in. *Let the games begin.*

Chapter 5

It was a raucous affair. What started as a small shindig for Tom turned into an all-out booze-fest. Too many double shifts and a lot of steam to vent. When he had a chance, Matt took Jamie aside.

"Hey, how's things in HLP?" Matt put his hands up near his face and did the old fly in the web *"Help Me"* from the original The Fly movie.

Jamie rolled his eyes, but smiled. "Man, that is getting old."

Matt chuckled. "So, I heard something. A rumor that the new hiber units have some problems."

"Where did you hear that?" Jamie asked, suddenly serious, leaning into Matt.

"Oh, just around. The main thing is that I hear they aren't being recalled."

Jamie went slightly red. "Jesus, I don't know what you're talking about." He got a bit shifty, looking everywhere but at Matt.

"You are a bad liar, dude. What's going on up there?"

Jamie came in close to Matt and spoke in a quiet voice. "Look, you can't say anything, but word from R&D is there's a significant failure rate with the hiberchamber testing. We reported it up the chain, but were told to keep our mouths shut and just install the damn things. But, you didn't hear that from me, man."

"*Acceptable Human Losses*. My dad used to tell me about that. They did their math and figured that the risk was acceptable. Heartless bastards."

Jamie looked into his beer. "Look, I just keep my head down and do what I'm told. I can't lose this job. You know what it's like out there for us Displaced."

"Yeah, I know. I know." Matt patted him on the shoulder. "Listen, don't sweat it. There's nothing that you can do, right?"

"Right." Jamie turned and shuffled off to his

HLP buddies.

Chapter 6

So, now it was confirmed. Matt was thinking of ways that he could get hold of Jonas without getting his friend into trouble - consorting with the help might raise some eyebrows. He decided to take a chance even though he knew that all calls were routinely scanned.

Matt pinged Jonas. He connected right away, his holo materializing in front of Matt's eyes.

"Hey, buddy," Matt said, "I was just thinking about home. Remember that time that we went up the Space Needle and you puked once we got to the top? That elevator totally messed you up."

"How could I ever forget. You'll never let me. But no one goes up there anymore."

"Yeah, well, I just wanted you to know that *I confirmed what you told me* about the authorities declaring some of those areas clean again. Pretty cool, hey?" Matt had heard this on the news, but Jonas had never said any such thing, and Matt was hoping that he got the hint.

"That's great news, Matt. We should celebrate some time."

"Agreed. I'll call you again soon and we can set up a time to get together."

Matt logged off and took a deep breath. *That went okay, I think. Message received. Now I have to figure out what to do next.* Obviously, reporting the problem to HLP would be useless; they already knew. And going to the government would be pointless. They were all in Worldstar's pocket.

If even one of the Displaced was deemed expendable, that was unacceptable to Matt. The fact that a significant number of his people were at risk of dying in space, alone, was outrageous. He owed it to the memory of his father and the rest of the Displaced to act. The fire in his belly was reignited.

Chapter 7

Jamie was busy working on a tricky circuit and didn't see the two big hulks until they were right on top of him. Grabbing an arm each, they yanked him away from his work desk.

"Hey, what the fuck guys! I've been working on that for hours."

"Shut up and listen," one of the guys barked, veins bulging in his neck. "Just want to have a little chat about them hibernation units."

The other guy piped in with, "We're just doing a little check around to make sure that all you mice aren't squeakin'. You know what I mean. Wouldn't want to have yourself a little *industrial accident*. Right?"

Jamie was shaking. "Hey guys, no problem. I just want to keep my job. You ain't gonna get any problems from me. No way."

The goons pushed him down harshly into his chair and glared at him. The bigger guy said, "You don't want to ever see us again. Ever." And they turned and left as quickly as they had arrived.

Jamie nearly crapped himself in fear. He started shaking all over. *Holy shit, what if they find out about what I told Matt. Me and my big mouth. Idiot. Idiot. Idiot.* He hit himself in the head a few times for good measure. After some time, he tried to get back to work, but couldn't. Now he was behind and would have to stay after work to meet quota. *Could this day get any worse?*

His eyephone chirped. It was Matt. *No way.* Jamie let it go to message.

Chapter 8

Matt had tried Jamie repeatedly for a few days and got nothing. They must have gotten to him somehow. *Does that mean I'm exposed too? Was I careless somehow?*

Matt paced around his little apartment. He had to figure out a way to get to HLP. Problem was that going higher up would only get him disappeared. *What about the press? That's just as dangerous, they're all controlled by Worldstar. Nothing gets out that isn't completely screened.*

After the terrorist attacks, the USA had instituted Marshall Law for a time. During that period legislation that was put in made the old *Patriot Act* look like child's play. Press freedoms were severely curtailed, surveillance of everyday citizens was increased, powers to hold people without trial were bolstered, and Homeland Security was given broad sweeping powers. Basically, the old George Orwell predictions had come true. Big Brother was certainly watching, and some animals were definitely more equal than others. But people accepted these changes out of fear, and there were no major challenges to the massive loss of civil rights. Even when Canada was made a US protectorate in the name of Homeland Security, the international community was too paralyzed to make any real protests. With nuclear war a real possibility, most nations were simply in survival mode.

Matt had to figure out a way to get on that hibernation work crew. *Time to call in some favors.*

Chapter 9

Jonas was waiting patiently for an elevator down to accounting on ninety-six and watching the numbers of one car slowly rise to one hundred. He heard the ding and waited for the doors to open. He wasn't expecting what came out. When she exited the elevator, his jaw nearly hit the floor. She was stunning. Long black hair, tall, gorgeous green eyes, and dressed in a very flattering power suit that accentuated her awesome legs.

"Jonas," said George from HR, whom Jonas didn't even notice was there at first, "this is Hanna. She was just flown in to oversee the final stages of the colony project. She's being set up in Craig's old office." Craig was a senior executive who recently took early retirement. *Probably sunning his fat ass in Nassau. Lucky bastard.*

"Nice to meet you, Hanna." Jonas shook her hand firmly. "Let me take it from here, George. I can show her around one hundred." George paused at first, shuffling from leg to leg, but when Jonas gave him a meaningful look he quickly handed the file he was holding over to Hanna.

"This has everything that you'll need, Hanna, to get started. All the login codes and office procedures. Welcome to Worldstar," and with that George turned and pushed the down button.

Jonas guided Hanna toward her office. "So, where did you come from?"

Hanna finally looked up from the file, as if noticing Jonas for the first time. "Jonas, right. Listen, I am here for one purpose and one purpose only. To make sure that these launches happen on time, and more importantly, on budget. This project is too important. So, you will excuse me if I don't have time to engage in small talk."

Jonas was lost for words. "Well, then… ah… Hanna, here is your office. Hope you settle in well."

Jonas turned on his heel and bee-lined back to the elevator. *What a ball buster. But, man is she hot.* Jonas smiled. His new life mission was to break through that ice.

Chapter 10

Gordon got the Earth-side flash on his eyephone mid-breakfast paste squirt, and nearly choked on the goop. He tapped his implant and immediately saw Matt, his old buddy from New Dallas.

"Gordon! How's things man!" Matt exclaimed.

Gordon managed to gulp down his mouthful. "Just enjoying a lovely meal of bacon and eggs in a tube. Yummy. What's up, this call must be costing you a fortune."

"Don't worry about that. Hey, any chance that you can get me up to work on those deep space cruisers?"

"What, you actually want to be transferred up here? You know that I was demoted for that fight with the super. I'll be stuck in this tin can for months."

"Yeah, I need to get out of here for awhile, lay low. Can you get me on the crew? You owe me one for that time…"

"Dude, the walls have ears," Gordon interrupted. "I remember. Just don't know if I actually am doing you a favor."

"Well, I would consider us even, buddy."

"Seems like a no brainer for me. Flash me your file and I'll put in for the transfer and transport on the next hyper."

Matt tapped off and flashed his data pack to Gordon. Now he would just have to improvise how to deal with the HLP hibernation units when he got up there.

Chapter 11

Hanna recalculated the projected human losses on the deep space flight to the Mars colony. It was presently at five percent, but as the project was nearing completion this figure was rising, and even the Company had its limits.

Unfortunately, the launch window was very tight. Mars was nearing its closest point to Earth, known as "opposition," which only happened every two years. The travel time to Mars in the colonial ship would be approximately three hundred days. Given the size of the vessel and the energy that was needed to make the journey, there was no way to get there any faster. The 2020 Viking III mission had made the journey in a record one hundred and ninety-nine days, but that was a small ship. This was followed by the first manned mission to Mars in 2026. The world cheered as man stepped down on the red planet; except this time it was a woman, Commander Janice Strong, who uttered the now famous words, "Mankind has just stepped into the future," giving homage to Neil Armstrong's legendary words when making that fateful leap onto the surface of the Moon.

This successful mission led to more and more ambitious journeys to our second closest cousin, the first closest being inhospitable Venus. Private companies were able to make a business model for exploration. In fact, it was FLX Energy's subsidiary, FLX Space Mining, whose near-Earth-asteroid and Moon operations had not only provided the raw materials for all of the orbital stations and spacecraft, but had also financed the entire Mars colonization project. With Earth energy, mineral, and precious metal resources running low, FLX Space Mining was able to generate trillions of dollars in revenue from the mining operations. In January 2048, FLX Space Mining launched the first of a series of Mars vessels designed to build mining colonies, developed by Worldstar. A successful Mars colonization would create untold profit for the Company, and therefore its shareholders.

Unknown to the common man, gene-nanobot technology had already extended life for the very rich to possibly hundreds of years. A point of a percent of humanity was on the cusp of near immortality, and limitless power and wealth. Hanna's purpose for existence was to ensure that the aims and goals of this elite were met.

Mr. Kerr, the hapless CEO, had called an executive meeting to introduce Hanna to the team. She waited until they were all seated before she made her entrance. Hanna meant to make her presence known.

"Gentleman and ladies. I am Hanna Smith, and I have been brought in to get the space colony program back on track." Hanna used her implant to project some three-dimensional graphs and spreadsheets just above the middle of the large boardroom table. *These should be simplified enough for these dimwits.* "As you can see, efficiencies are dropping due to ineffective cost-cutting measures. This will stop now. To start, I am eliminating thirty senior and mid-level managers. Their jobs are redundant and can be absorbed by the other managers. Further, we need more work from our labor force. All vacations are now frozen until final delivery of all components are made to space port."

Hanna looked around at the stunned silence. No one knew if their head was on the chopping block. No point sticking your neck out.

Jonas didn't see it that way. This was his chance to act. "If we do this, the workers might get unruly. We need to have a plan to deal with that. Also, have you thought how we should handle the firings?"

"Jonas, right?" Hanna looked at her tablet, though she knew who he was and his background. "Graduated from MIT Business School, worked for Telsun Communications before being headhunted by WorldStar. Worked your way up to VP of Space Vacation division. Give me one good reason that you should stay?"

Everyone turned to Jonas. Mr. Kerr had a smirk on his face. Jonas turned beet red but got up the courage to say, "I am willing to do whatever it takes to make sure that WorldStar is profitable."

Hanna nodded and turned to the other management team. "I will be meeting with you all individually to assess whether you fit into the new WorldStar business model." And with that, Hanna turned and exited the boardroom.

One of the senior project managers looked at Mr. Kerr. "Can she do that?"

Mr. Kerr's forehead was starting to bead with sweat. "Yes. Yes, she can."

Chapter 12

"It's your lucky day, Matt. I think. Corporate is trying to ramp the project up and wants three more bodies up here. So looks like you, Sandy Parker, and Parm Singh are heading up on the next shuttle. Pack your bags, my friend!" Gordon seemed happy that he was getting some new company top-side.

"Thanks for getting me in there. I'll see you soon." Matt tapped off and immediately started to throw his meager possessions into the small duffle allowed for the trip.

The next hyper was in two days. *Okay, now what. I need a plan.*

Chapter 13

Sandy was mad as hell. "WTF with this transfer shit. What did I do to get shipped out?"

"You're too good at your job, Sandy," Matt explained. "They need the best up there. Hey, they nabbed Parm, too. He's a hotshot engineer." That seemed to mollify Sandy somewhat. She just grumbled under her breath and threw her travel sack onto the security conveyer. Security guards waived her into the body scan and then she was sprayed down with decontamination chemicals.

Parm came running up the ramp to the employee security check-in point. He was pouring with sweat. Matt and Sandy looked back as he scrambled to get his items in order.

"Let's go," Matt chirped with a laugh, "don't want to be late for your funeral."

Parm looked up in clear distress. "I design and build these things. I don't fly in them."

"Hyper flight is safer than walking down the street in New Dallas," Sandy shouted back through the contamination mist.

"That's supposed to make me feel better?" Parm was obviously not amused.

"You'll be fine. Or you won't. That's life," Matt said sarcastically.

After about fifteen minutes, the three amigos were walking towards the boarding lobby for the workhorse *WorldStar Spacejet V3-X*. In its prime this machine had been cutting edge technology, pushing the boundaries of consumer Earth-space travel. Now, instead of carrying twenty-four passengers, it carried mostly cargo and up to six space dock workers. The V3-X was able to take off and land like a normal jet, but was engineered to reach low-Earth orbit and dock with space stations. It took decades to achieve this engineering marvel. But as with so many other seemingly insurmountable challenges, like landing a man on the moon or curing HIV-AIDS, human ingenuity prevailed.

Chapter 14

Jonas was sitting in Hanna's office. She had kept him waiting for fifteen minutes before he was ushered in, and now she sat there without saying a word. Even though he was completely shitting himself inside, Jonas had used the time waiting to calm his nerves, and seemed outwardly at ease. He decided to be patient and see what she had up her sleeve. *Hey, there's nothing I can do anyway.*

Hanna finally looked up from her virtudesk. "So, Jonas, what are we going to do with you?"

"What do you have in mind?" Jonas calmly replied. He tried to keep his expression neutral. *Don't want to come off as an ass.*

"I have read through all of your records and you have done well working your way up the ladder at WorldStar. What do you think of the space vacation sector?"

"Technology is better. Price point is down. Access is up. It has massive growth potential."

"Yes, well, what about you? Do you want to stay in space holidays for the rest of your career?"

"I'm happy to go wherever I'm needed."

"Hm, wherever? That may be a bit prophetic."

"What do you mean?"

"I want you up top overseeing the colony project, reporting directly to me. You will be given the title of COO of the Space Colony Division. Do you want it?"

Jonas' heart was pounding in his chest. Up top, in space? COO? What about Randy Thompson? "Can I think about it?"

"I don't have time to mess around. I am holding a shuttle right now. Everything that you need is in a bag outside this office. Instructions have been sent to your pad. It is that or the alternative." And Hanna slowly pushed forward a pile of formal legal documents; he could see the big title Severance Package.

"Well, in that case. Let's do it." Jonas smiled broadly, but inside his mind was racing.

Chapter 15

What is the hold up? Matt was getting impatient as they sat for hours on the tarmac. Of course, Parm was losing his mind, which made matters much worse. The pilot came on periodically saying that there had been a short delay and that they would get going shortly. *Blah, blah, blah.*

Then the hatch re-opened, and to Matt's shock Jonas walked in looking like he had lost his pet snake.

Jonas saw Matt as he sat down, and his forehead crinkled in a frown. "What the hell are you doing here, Matt?"

"I was just going to ask you the same thing."

"Heads are rolling in the tower. Some high-powered exec came in and she's shaking everything up. She gave me a huge promotion… I think. Anyway, turns out I'm the new COO of Space Colony. Maybe she was trying to get back at me for hitting on her? Maybe she thinks I can do a better job? Who knows?"

Matt chuckled. "Looks like we're all in the doghouse. Jonas, this is Sandy and Parm." Sandy glowered back at Jonas and Parm put on a brave face, green at the gills.

"Well, we're a sorry lot, aren't we?" Jonas got strapped in as the safety announcements came on.

The entertainment system came on and a cheery, blonde female flight attendant explained, "In the case of an emergency, please don your helmets and ensure that emergency oxygen is established. Your seat is equipped with an ejection system that will only deploy if you are fully locked in and all systems are operational. In the case of a water landing, please find inflatable…

More like, in the case of emergency bend over and kiss your ass goodbye, thought Matt.

The take-off and initial acceleration were uneventful. It was only when the hyper-engines kicked in that Matt really understood the power of this machine; to get to escape velocity, the spaceplane had to pull some serious Gs. Matt managed to turn his head enough to see Parm. *Poor guy, he's in his own personal hell right now.* Then, after what seemed an eternity, they were suddenly weightless. Matt was feeling a bit queasy, and Parm was obviously feeling a lot worse. Or at least from the retching, that was what it sounded like.

The V3-X approached the space dock. It was awe inspiring to see the Earth below, all blue and beautiful. So different from the reality of the scorched earth of Seattle. His home. Above, or below depending on your perspective, the massive space dock came into view, with the hulking nuclear-thermal rocket-propelled space colony ship clinging to its underbelly. They could read *Colonial I* on the prow of the vessel. Robotic arms danced over the surface of the ship, securing God-knows-what parts to the ever-growing vessel. Not the prettiest sight, but in space there was no need for aerodynamics.

The spaceplane maneuvered closer and closer to the dock. Matt looked out at his new home. *Good times.*

Chapter 16

Mr. Kerr sat at his desk with Hanna opposite him. She was sitting very calmly, cool and collected. *Like a bloody cobra, ready to strike.*

"Bob, you have been a very valuable asset to the Company. Of course, we didn't appreciate having to come down here and get your ship in order, but nonetheless, you understand your role and you play it well. So, for the time being, you will stay on as CEO and oversee the changes that have been instituted. Are there any problems with that?"

"No… absolutely not. All we want is to make sure that the shareholders are happy and that WorldStar is profitable." Mr. Kerr glanced at his fishing holiday vid, wishing he were there right now.

"Good. Well, my job is nearly done here. I plan on going up top once Jonas is settled, to make sure that the colony plans are completed as per our requirements. *I* will tidy up the last of the downsizing measures. If *you* can please put pressure on your supers to get the workers to improve their productivity, then everything will be copasetic."

Without another word, Hanna got up and marched out of the office. Mr. Kerr remembered suddenly to breathe. *Maybe the golden parachute would have been preferable to this crap.*

Chapter 17

Dr. Little looked up from his microscope. Below him on the OR table was another recipient of a new version of the nanobot therapy. He was responding well. Adjustments to the treatment were resulting in fewer rejections, but they were still unacceptably high. Since he had received the therapy himself, the doctor's mental acuity had increased exponentially, and his stamina had become nearly super-human. Even more importantly, the nagging ethical dilemma that he used to have in regard to the research was gone - he could focus completely on his work. He perceived the patient fatalities more as a personal failure in his research. He felt nothing for them as individuals. *They knew the risks. They understood that the gamble could result in either near immortality or death. They signed the waivers.*

Above, in the observation area, Gregory Hicks' ghostly holoprojection looked on. R&D had added some new variants to the therapy. The treatment had been safe for some time in its basic form, but longevity and enhanced intellect were not enough. The Company needed compliance; a population that was completely obedient, but unaware that it was being manipulated. It was this variation that was causing the biggest problems. *These drones are far too mentally rebellious.*

Suddenly, the bells started ringing and the patient started to spasm uncontrollably. Nurses jumped in and tried to control the procedure, but it was too late. Another loss. *Another failure. Unacceptable.* Hick's ghostly apparition flicked off.

PART II Up Top

It was breathtaking to see how quickly giant corporations like FLX Energy were able to dominate mining in outer space. The real space race began when companies began making claims to planets and asteroids. International law concerning space exploration, started through treaties such as the Outer Space treaty of 1967 and the Moon Treaty of 1979, had deemed outer space to be the common heritage of all mankind, like Antarctica. The problem was that all of these treaties were between nation states and were not strictly applicable to multi-national corporations. This loophole was exploited to its maximum when energy and mineral resources began to seriously dwindle in the 2020s. The international community simple stepped aside. Once mobilized, the large energy companies and their subsequent cartel, the Company, created a multi-trillion dollar per annum business empire. **- Cassandra Taylor, chief colonial historian**

Chapter 1

Matt had never been claustrophobic, but the worker accommodations weren't exactly luxurious. Utilitarian, efficient, dorm style. Coffins stacked on top of each other, four deep on each side of the corridor. Shared meals. Shared showers. No privacy. *What have I gotten myself into?*

Artificial gravity allowed the crew to function relatively normally inside the crew quarters and the basic workstations, but other than that, everything was zero g. That meant everyone had to have a strict workout regime, and supplements were required to keep their muscles from atrophying and bones from weakening.

Matt looked out from the crowded mess through the portal. While the station was constantly spinning to create artificial gravity, the windows only displayed a snap shot from each rotation, giving the illusion of the dock being stationary. Directly across from the worker station he could see the corporate accommodations module. From what he heard, basically everything that they didn't have, corporate had in spades. Matt pictured

Jonas lying on a lounging chair being fed grapes by a gorgeous hostess. *Bastard.* He shook his head to clear it.

Focus, dude. Get your shit together. Matt turned back to the canteen and took a look at the motley crew that that made up the work detail. He sighed. *Show time.*

Parm and Sandy were arguing about the construction slowdowns.

"Bad design, that's what it is," Sandy said. "You computer nerds don't think like people. Nothing functions in a way that a normal human being would use it. Then we have to tweak things so that they work."

"If you just built to spec, we wouldn't be behind schedule," Parm exclaimed with some clear frustration.

And on and on the argument went. It had started as soon as they arrived and kept going in one form or another. Other crew and tech staff just looked down into their breakfast mush bowls and stayed clear of it.

"Okay, you two," Matt said, "lay off. This is getting boring. We have to get to work and figure out a way to get this project back on track, or heads are going to roll."

Sandy looked up at Matt and was about to say something, but had a second thought. Sandy was tough, and Matt had always found her to be really attractive. He liked strong women, and Sandy was all that. Matt grinned and pointed down the shaft towards the workstations.

"Eat up, you two. We've got to get a move on. Those hiberchambers aren't going to build themselves," Matt went on. Even though Matt had been brought in to help on the hibernation modules, it was the hardware he was working on, not the software. He knew that it was somewhere in the meds or the computer program that the problem must lie. At least he was here and could try and figure out what to do. In the meantime, he had a schedule to keep.

Chapter 2

Jonas rubbed his eyes. He had been getting very little sleep since arriving at the space dock. As the COO he had huge responsibilities, and he had to figure out how to get the project back on schedule. They had installed only five hundred and sixty-eight of the thousand hiberchambers and the rate that the units were being completed at was at a crawl. He had to get to the bottom of the problem. To make matters worse, Hanna was coming up in a week to inspect the situation.

Another team leader meeting. Endless meetings. What he needed was action, not excuses. *I need to talk to Matt, he'll know how to fix this thing. He should be where I am.* Jonas pictured his buddy in the workshops, sweating over his workstation with some angry super breathing down his neck. *Maybe it's time for a tour of the facility.* Jonas hit the intercom and asked his assistant to set up an immediate spot inspection of the workstations.

Chapter 3

Zone D's hatch opened and Jonas walked out onto the work floor. The factory layout meant that each hiberchamber was passed by dozens of specialists, each of whom installed their specific parts. It could be a manufacturing facility anywhere on Earth, only they were miles above the planet's surface. As Jonas walked through the stations a fawning super came running up in clear distress.

"Sir, we had no notice that you were coming. What a pleasant surprise," he smiled, but with a tone that evidenced his real meaning. "Craig Spinner, is my name."

Jonas inwardly cringed. *Sycophantic ass.* He simply nodded back.

Not knowing what to do, the super went on. "Let me show you around the floor. As you can see the crew is working very hard to get back on schedule." He gestured broadly with his arm to encompass the entire floor.

"Listen Craig, I don't have a lot of time. Why do we have people doing this work and not robotics? Surely, that would be more efficient?" Jonas knew the answer, but he wanted Craig to squirm a bit.

"Management told us that the cost benefit analysis showed that human labor was cheaper once you factored in the cost of transporting the heavy machinery up top. Also, human crews are more easily adaptable to changing manufacturing needs. But, robots *are* responsible for the bulk of the heavy lifting ship construction. I'm sure that you saw that on your way in."

"Yes, well, let's have a look around."

Craig went on nattering about this and that while Jonas tuned him out, looking for Matt. Finally he saw him down the third row. So as not to be obvious, Jonas stopped in front of a random workstation.

Interrupting Craig's droning, Jonas asked the worker, "So what's your job?"

The worker hadn't noticed them coming, he was concentrating so hard. Looking up from his desk, he saw the super and Jonas and barely managed to stutter out, "S-s-s-ystem relays, sir. I'm installing system relays."

"Very good. Carry on, son."

Jonas made his way to Matt's station. He stopped there and wasn't sure what to do. It wouldn't be a good idea to tip his hand to the super that Matt and he were school chums; that would make Matt's life a living hell up here. Instead, he had brought over a written note with his private in-house access code. He was breaking every protocol giving this code up, but he really needed to get some inside help. "So, what are you working on?"

Matt looked up and Jonas gave him a little wink. "I'm installing the medical delivery system." He picked up what looked like a hydra's head and handed it to Jonas to have a look. Tubes and connectors covered the device. It looked scary. Jonas made sure that his note was attached to the device so that only Matt could see it as he handed it back.

"Very good work." Jonas turned to Craig. "Well, I've seen enough for now. Looks like your crew is working hard, but word from above is that we have to pick up the pace. So, can I count on you to get this crew producing faster?" Jonas looked hard at Craig who started nodding furiously.

"Yes, sir. We will increase efficiency. Just you wait and see."

As Jonas walked back to the hatch door, he could hear Craig behind him starting to yell at his crew to pick up the slack. Jonas smiled to himself. *Some things never change.*

Chapter 4

Matt looked at the note. All it had was a number, but he knew immediately what it was. A proprietary communication code. *Why would Jonas risk giving this out to a worker? He must be deep into something. But, Jonas knows that if I use this, it can be traced to me. He knows that I know this and he needs me to figure out a workaround.*

Matt memorized the number and destroyed the note. He got back to work, but his mind was distracted.

Chapter 5

Parm had been on the team that designed the delivery system for the hiberchamber meds and nutrition. R&D at Worldstar had developed a nanobot system that regulated body functions to put the occupant of the unit into a perfect hibernation state. This was regulated by a complex computer system that constantly communicated with the nanobots, ensuring that the person in the unit was safe and properly nourished. Parm's delivery system was the interface between the computer and the occupant. It had to operate flawlessly. There was no room for error.

Parm worked in the final testing area for the units. He ran diagnostics and was responsible for passing or failing the units before installation into the ship. There was a lot of pressure to approve the units. His predecessor had ended his up-top shift early for some reason that no one seemed willing to talk about, so Parm had been rushed up to take his place.

Parm had heard the rumors of faulty units being installed, but he didn't believe it. *Who would do that? We're talking about human lives here.*

What Parm noticed almost immediately was that the units being completed had been slightly altered from their original design. Cheaper components had been substituted in some areas, resulting in possible weak links in the system. So far, his tests had resulted in a number of possible system failures that meant that units were being sent back to the floor.

At the end of his shift, Craig Spinner made his way over and waived him into his office. "Office" was actually a kind word for a tiny cubby-hole with a sliding door. The main thing was that it allowed for some privacy.

"Parm, how are you adjusting to being up top?"

"It has taken some time, but I have resigned myself to the inevitability of death. It keeps me calm."

"Well, okay then... Listen, you've been sending units back to the floor. You know we're behind on our quota."

"If a system fails the tests, I am going to send it back. I care about human safety, not quotas."

"Spoken like a good quality control specialist. Great. But I reviewed your findings and I think that you're being a bit too picky with the testing. Just because the tests show a *possibility* of failure, doesn't mean that there will be *actual* failure."

"I was on the original design team. The final product does not match our design specs, and therefore there are potential weaknesses presenting. Some of the components are testing as insufficiently robust to handle deep space flight. They need to be replaced. I do not accept any margin for error."

"Hmm, well, thanks for your time." Craig stood up and put out his hand, and smiled.

Parm was a bit confused, but got up, turned around, and pushed the button to activate the door. Frowning, he walked back to the mess. *What is going on up here?*

Chapter 6

The mess was crowded and the work crew was always boisterous, outspoken with their opinions about the world down below. No one worried about the surveillance; there was no point fighting it. Just as they had become accustomed to it down below, they threw caution to the wind.

"Protectorate my ass. We were annexed. Call it what you will, but we suddenly became the fifty-first state with less rights than Puerto Rico," said Carter Williams, one of the Toronto Displaced. Carter was one of thousands of Canadians who were offered work permits to help build New Dallas and the spaceport. With the worldwide economic meltdown that happened after 911-2, many Canadian Displaced made their way south with the hope of jobs.

"Come on, Carter, what do you expect? The terrorists got in through the Canadian border. We had to protect our cities from further attacks," Gordon piped in.

"You still believe that crap, eh? There's no proof that the bombs came through Canada.

That was just your jingoistic press spouting garbage," Carter went on.

"Oh, so you're one of those conspiracy theory guys?" Sandy asked with a smirk, knowing full-well that she was putting a red flag up to a bull.

A voice from across the room shouted, "You should count yourself lucky, Canucklehead!" Laughter and hoots erupted around the mess.

You could see Carter's face get redder and redder as his passions started to overtake his intellect. Matt saw where this was going and put a hand on Carter's shoulder.

"It's not worth it, buddy, let it go," Matt said.

Carter was clearly seething, but he just put his head down and concentrated on the lovely slop they called chow.

After he was sure that things wasn't going to escalate, Matt turned to Sandy. "So, how are you settling in?"

"Well, my hair is a mess and I need a manicure," Sandy said sarcastically. "Seriously,

Matt, I'm just trying to log my time and meet my quotas so that I can get back down below."

"I know how you feel. They didn't design the workers' modules for comfort, that's for sure." Matt glanced down the row and saw Parm. He had his head down and was eating quietly.

"What's up with Parm? He's usually bellyaching about something."

"Not sure, he's been really quite for the last few days."

Matt picked up his empty tray and threw it in the recycling machine, then grabbed a cup of what they said was coffee for himself and Parm. He sat down next to him and put an arm on his shoulder.

"Hey Parm. What's shaking dude?"

Parm squirmed uncomfortably and tried to get out of Matt's embrace. Matt could see that Parm was obviously not a happy camper, and tried another tack. He removed his arm and placed the coffee in front of him.

"I prefer tea," Parm said, "but thanks."

"That's it? That's all you got? Where's the Parm I know?"

"Don't really want to talk right now. Maybe you could just leave me alone?"

Matt was confused. Parm was never like this. Something had to be up, and Matt realized that he wasn't going to get anything out of Parm in the crowded mess hall.

"Okay, Parm. But listen, I need to talk to you about something. Can you meet me at my work station in ten?"

 "Okay then," Parm said with a sigh of resignation.

Chapter 7

Gregory Hicks was enjoying a nice cigar and brandy in his massive penthouse suite overlooking Central Park in Manhattan. He had more money than God and loved that he wouldn't have to give it away to any sniveling offspring. He would outlive his current wife and his two obnoxious brats. He could eat, drink, smoke, and fuck all that he wanted, and his body would automatically compensate for any impurities or overindulgences. *Life is good, very good.*

Being the CEO and major shareholder of one of the biggest energy companies in the world certainly had its benefits. FLX Energy had started modestly fifty years earlier with a few oil wells, and had slowly grown, gobbling up other energy companies until its revenues were in the tens of billions of dollars per year. FLX Energy had subsidiary companies in space industry, mining, LNG, health care, even pharmaceuticals.

Ten years earlier, one of their Swiss drug companies had contacted Gregory with an offer he could not refuse. In exchange for a massive future R&D budget, Deccapharm had agreed to provide a combination of gene and nanobot therapy treatment to the senior executives of FLX Energy and its subsidiaries. After reviewing the impeccable Swiss research and testing reports, Gregory had to admit that this was nothing short of miraculous.

As it turned out, in those early days the procedure was very complex. Using a large corporate strategic planning session as a cover, the senior execs all set off to Switzerland for a two-week stay in the Deccapharm facility. First, the patients had to be put into an induced comma. Next, the gene therapy. This part of the treatment literally turned off the aging gene that was nature's way of controlling the population. Finally, nanobots were introduced into the bloodstream. Millions of microscopic smart machines with specific tasks regulated every part of the body, quickly fixing problems from attacking viruses, to mending clogged arteries, to connecting brain synapses, to killing cancer cells. The nanobots never stopped working.

Gregory had read every word of the NDA and waiver, and had realized that there was some risk with the procedure. But it was worth it.

Near immortality? Wasn't that what every person truly wished for?

Only one of the twenty executives succumbed during the therapy. Poor old Gerry hadn't made it. *He was an asshole anyway. Good riddance.*

Gregory had also come away from the experience with a new thought. What if the nanobots could be used in other ways? What if they could be used to control people? Gregory envisioned an army of completely compliant workers. The thought made him smile.

Chapter 8

While Matt waited for Parm to show up, he calmly contemplated his options. Was it time to trust someone else with this knowledge? Or would that just mean that Parm would become vulnerable too? He could sure use Parm's brains on the Jonas communication code issue. While he was still thinking, Parm tapped him on the shoulder. Startled, Matt turned around in his chair.

"Man, that was stealthy. I didn't hear you coming."

"If the heart be impure, all actions will be wrong," Parm said cryptically.

Matt furrowed his brow. "What does that mean?"

"I don't know. It was on a fridge magnet at my parent's house," Parm said, looking down at his feet.

"You are one weird character, Parm." Matt made up his mind. "Listen, there's something you need to know." He turned on his compressor and got Parm to lean in. He told

Parm the story of the faulty units, including Jonas' trip to his place, Jamie's confirmation, and this trip up top.

Parm didn't say anything, just listened and nodded quietly. Speaking closely into Matt's ear so as not to be overheard, he said, "Matt, I can tell you that there are indeed some problems with the hiberchambers. If we do not fix some of the components, people will most surely die in deep space. I thought that I was alone with this knowledge, but it helps to know that I can share this burden with you as well."

Matt went on to explain that Jonas was actually up top with them and wanted to try and contact them. He said that he had Jonas' proprietary company code, but didn't know how to use it without being traced.

Parm thought a moment, then said, "Leave it with me. I will figure out a workaround. In the meantime, we need to figure out how we can slow down work-flow until we figure out a way to fix these units. I will not be an accomplice to the murder of my fellow Displaced."

"Okay, let's figure out a way to meet up tomorrow without drawing attention," said Matt.

"Leave that to me," said Parm. He turned and walked away like a man with a mission.

Chapter 9

Jonas had been waiting for a call from Matt, and he was losing patience. *How hard is it to figure out a way to make the call?* He only had a week until the wicked witch of the north came a-calling. He needed answers about what was holding things up on the floor. He had met with everyone on the management team, and for the most part the ship was well on its way to being completed. The robotic construction team was on-time and on-budget for the ship structure. It was just the interior, and particularly the hiberchambers, that were holding things up. There was too high a rejection rate, too many units coming back to the floor.

Jonas' private eyephone pinged. He tapped in and Matt's face came up.

"I have less than two minutes before this patch is compromised. What's so important that you need to risk us both losing our jobs?"

"Look, I need to know what the problem is on the floor. The ice queen will be arriving next week, and I need answers."

Matt glanced at his watch, keeping an eye on the ticking seconds. "You know damn well what the problem is. You told me yourself that some of the units were failing. Corporate cheaped out on components, and some of the units aren't passing testing. Some are coming back to the floor, but supers are starting to let the marginal fails through. You have to stop this, we can't let any faulty units through."

Jonas was between a rock and a hard place. If he did the right thing and slowed production, he and his entire crew would be axed. If he pushed production with the present supplies, people would die in space. But if he did do the right thing, a new team would be up here pronto. Then he couldn't do anything and he would be out on his ass with no job.

Matt was glowering at him through the eyephone. He glanced at the time again. "Gotta go. I'll reestablish when I can," Matt said, then he signed off.

Jonas was nowhere farther ahead. *What am I going to do?*

Chapter 10

Selfish bastard. Jonas was only thinking of his own hide. Matt was pacing up and down the crew bunks corridor while everyone else was having dinner. He had no appetite.

Parm was a freakin' genius. He had engineered a brilliant patch to the communications system managing to splice it directly into Matt's eyephone. It was tied somehow to the diagnostic system, which ran on two-minute cycles. He could only risk using it intermittently, as any pattern might get picked up by the onboard computer system.

Centuries before, Luddites had broken weaving frames to protest new labor-saving technologies in textiles that would lead job losses. As the story went, their hero, Ned Ludd, had broken two frames in a fit of passion after being whipped for idleness. A "Luddite" became anyone who was against technological progress. Matt remembered hearing the story from his father, who had explained that getting too stuck in any job was a mistake. The only thing constant in this world was change. At the same time, his father had also felt strongly that even in changing work environments, workers needed to be treated with respect and dignity. Matt's father was a strong believer in the strength of the now outlawed union movement.

The problem with organizing some kind of protest was that they were in outer space, and completely at the mercy of the great Worldstar corporation. The construction module that they were in could easily be separated from the main orbiting dock. Matt could imagine the headlines announcing the deaths of the valiant workers on one of mankind's most ambitious projects. He could hear the pundits now, talking about the loss of life on most big projects, but how these space workers were heroes etc. etc. They would be a blip on a footnote in history.

No, Matt had to be smarter than that. All of these people were vulnerable; the company had them and their families over a barrel.

"Hey Matt. What's up with you?" Sandy asked. She had just finished her mandatory workout, and Matt found himself momentarily distracted from his deep thoughts. *Man, she is cute.* He couldn't help himself. He had always had a thing for Sandy, but had never had the courage to pursue it. She had always seemed out of his league.

"Nothing," Matt said as he felt the blood rush to his face.

"Nothing, my ass," Sandy said. "You've been brooding since we got here. You need to chill a bit."

Matt considered telling Sandy what was going on, but he didn't want word getting around that there was a serious problem on the floor.

"It's like you said. I just want to do my eight month shift and get back down."

"Well, you aren't going to make it if you keep this up. Listen, a few of us have a card game going. You should jump in."

Matt let out a deep breath, closed his eyes, and then realized that Sandy was right. He had to take it down a notch. Looking up at Sandy, he said, "Yeah, that would be fun."

"Okay then, let's go."

Matt followed Sandy back to the mess, where a game of poker was in progress. Parm was looking on quietly.

"Hey, Matty. Ready to lose your shirt?" Carter asked with a grin.

Matt turned to Sandy. "Are you setting me up?"

"The grift is on." Sandy winked and gave her best coquettish smile.

Matt shook his head and had a chuckle. *I'm such an idiot. These are my people. I'm not in this alone.*

"Deal me in, suckers."

Chapter 11

Gregory Hicks used his handprint and an optical scan to get access to the reception area of the secret U.S.-based research facility. As he walked in, obsequious staff immediately greeted him. He rarely had to visit this lab in person, but when he did the little rats would scurry. *Who could work like this?* He never knew how the science nerds did it. Within a few seconds, Dr. Little greeted him at reception and walked with him back to his office.

Once the door was shut and they were seated, Dr. Little started. "Good to see you. Mr. Hicks. I hope that you're well?"

"Seriously, Little… small talk? Where are we with this new treatment?" Gregory Hicks snapped, relishing in making Dr. Little jump to his command.

"Well, sir, you know that the variations on the original Swiss formula have run into some issues. We haven't had any successful tests, and I'm worried that the number of missing employees will start being noticed."

"They're being selected from all over the planet, right? Who's going to know?"

"True. True. But, we have to be careful nonetheless."

"Fair enough. So, what's the problem?"

"It seems that there are parts of the brain that are particularly resistant to the nanobot insertion. It's part of our hard-wired survival instinct. The nanobots seem to trigger an uncontrollable response from the hypothalamus, resulting in an extreme adrenaline release. This results in massive heart failure. Essentially, we're triggering a fear response that is so intense that the subjects die."

"Hmm. Well, can't you just have a secondary nanobot regulate the hypothalamus?"

"Yes, we have tried that. We're getting close, but we need more time. The brain seems to revert to a primitive response that is very difficult to regulate."

"We don't have time. Colonial I will be ready for launch in less than eight months, and we need to have a fully operational control system for the colonists. You understand what's at stake here. We can't have a ship full of unruly and uncontrolled workers. Ramp it up. I want this problem solved."

"Yes sir." And that was the end of that discussion.

"And how is Phase 2 going? We need these systems to be able to transfer in utero so that offspring are also compliant."

"We are confident that we can create specialized nanobots for that purpose, but we need a test subject who has already been successfully treated. Once pregnant, we would simply wait until the fetus is viable, say six months, and then introduce the treatment."

Gregory only had to think for an instant to come up with the perfect candidate. He activated his eyephone and clicked on the contact.

"Hanna, how is my favorite prodigy? Listen, I have another assignment for you."

Chapter 12

Sandy wondered if Matt would ever figure out how she felt about him. He seemed blind to her advances, always so serious and preoccupied. But she knew that under that seemingly tough exterior was a heart of gold. She was sick of the losers that she had hooked up with in the past. They didn't care about her, they only wanted to get some action. *Well I need some action, too!*

Sandy sighed and turned her head to stare down through the common room portal at Earth's beautiful blue surface. She could easily imagine Dallas still being there instead of the black crater that existed in its place. Instead of twisted metal and debris, new students were taking her place on the cheerleader squad. Sandy could hear the huge and crazy crowd on the home field at her high school; the near religious fervor of football fans in her city.

Why had she been in Fort Worth the day that the bomb went off? Why had the terrorists picked the day that they had an away game? Why had she been spared? She lost everything that day; her entire family and most of her friends. Even though she was lucky to be alive, she sometimes thought that she would have been better off if she could have died with them. It just hurt so much every day.

Sandy recalled the refuge camps with its tens of thousands of survivors; a year of fear and chaos, hopelessness and despair. Sandy could still picture the Worldstar trucks pulling up with the promise of a fresh start: the New Dallas spaceport - they could be part of the future. Sandy remembered throwing herself into the new work. It gave her life purpose again, and she had moved up quickly through the ranks. *If I had just punched the clock like everyone else, maybe I wouldn't have been recruited to go up top. Now I'm stuck in this shit hole.*

She was busy daydreaming when Matt came up behind her. "Hey Sandy," Matt said in a sheepish voice.

"Hey." Sandy turned, looked at Matt, and a smile came to her face. *Well, not everything is so bad up here.*

"I wanted to thank you for last night. I really needed to just let loose a bit with the guys. I've been a real drag lately, I know."

"No problem. I just thought you needed a good kick in the ass."

Matt chuckled. "Yeah, I guess I did." Without thinking what he was doing, Matt leaned in and gave Sandy a peck on the cheek.

Sandy, who was normally tough as nails, actually giggled and put her hand to her mouth. They both had a laugh.

"You know the company policy on fraternization, especially in space," Sandy said.

Matt sighed. "Yes, I know it well."

Sandy reached out and put her hand gently on Matt's arm. "It's really too bad..." She looked into his eyes and leaned in.

Matt suddenly became aware of the cameras that he knew were everywhere. Big Brother was always watching. He backed away and shifted his eyes up to the ceiling. Sandy nodded slightly, showing that she understood what he was saying.

Sandy's heart was pounding. *Where did that come from.*

Chapter 13

Hanna boarded the custom corporate spaceplane. This XTC-Mark II was the cutting edge of space travel; all of the comforts of a private jet with full low-orbital docking capabilities. An amazing feat of engineering. Hanna was the only passenger; a massive extravagance, but with her new mission she had priority.

The take-off and acceleration was incredibly exhilarating. New technologies dampened G-Forces for passenger comfort, but there was still an amazing feeling of velocity. As the Earth pulled away, Hanna considered her options. There were a number of eligible mates up top, but she thought that the best bet was Jonas. He was very attractive, so the assignment wouldn't be all that bad. She had to figure out how to play it. Hanna was well aware as to how intimidating she could be. She smiled to herself. She knew just how to play this. *It will be like taking candy from a baby.*

After ninety minutes, the spacedock could be seen in the distance. At first it was like another star, but as they got closer and closer the massive colony ship strapped to the dock came into focus. Hanna marveled at this project. It was truly awe-inspiring. The Company now had control of much of the Earth, but in order to get the unfettered room to grow that the Company truly needed, outer space was the only option. Hanna watched as the ballet of space docking took place.

Chapter 14

Jonas watched as the XTC-Mark II came into the dock. What an incredible machine. He craved that level of access. *How had Hanna gotten there so fast? She was probably younger than him, but she seemed to have risen to the top of the corporate structure. Judging by her icy personality, she probably didn't sleep her way to the top.*

Disembarking the spaceplane, Hanna swept into the holding area. She was dressed in the form fitting pressure suit that was mandatory for space travel. Jonas had a hard time keeping his mouth from hitting the floor. *Man, she is stunning.*

"Jonas, status report," she said, jumping right to business. *Then she opens her mouth.* Jonas sighed to himself, and then put on his best corporate smile.

"Right this way," *your highness,* "I have all of the production figures ready for your review."

Jonas ushered her into his office, where the holographic projectors were already showing the requisite graphs and charts tracking how construction was progressing. Everything looked great until they got to the section on the hiberchambers.

Hanna had already seen these figures, so there were no surprises, but she didn't want Jonas to know that. "I sent you up here to get production on track. It doesn't look like you've done that."

"Well, the basic issue is that I inherited a problem. Corporate has been so conscious about budget that some of the components are simply not up to design specs. Units are having to go back to the floor when these components fail testing."

"What I see is only marginally failing units being sent back. Just move the acceptable limit for passing the units."

"My projections show that if we do that, there will be a significant failure of units in deep space."

"These failures are within tolerable limits according to company policy."

Jonas hesitated slightly before continuing. A small bead of sweat slipped down his back as he made the decision to challenge Hanna. "Is that really acceptable? We're talking about human lives here."

Hanna paused, tipped her head a bit to the right and inspected Jonas for a minute. "Perhaps I made a mistake with you. I thought you said you would do what it took to get production on schedule?"

Jonas realized that he was on thin ice now. This was the dilemma that he knew was coming. He had thought about this a great deal over the past weeks, and he had a suggestion. He decided he had to take a chance. "How about another solution? Why don't we send a small work crew along with the ship? If a problem arises with any components, then they can be revived by the maintenance computer. That way, we can lower the pass threshold, launch the ship on time, *and* make sure that a maximum number of colonists are able to survive the trip."

Hanna pondered this idea. "Have you crunched the numbers on this proposal?"

Jonas was ready with his pitch – this is where he shone. *I could sell underwear to a nudist.*

Within a few minutes he had Hanna convinced. *It's up to you know, Matt.*

Just as he was finishing up Hanna reached out, touched his arm, and gave him a look that that was nearly approval. It was just a little gesture, but it sent electric jolts all over his body.

"So, now that we have a plan, where can a girl get something to eat?"

"The corporate dining room is fully appointed, and I think you'll be satisfied."

"I'm not sure about that. I am not easily satisfied," Hanna said with what Jonas could have sworn was a double meaning.

No, I'm just imagining things. "Would you like company?" Jonas asked.

"Sounds good. I need to change and freshen up, and I have some work to do. Let's say 1900 hours? Make sure that it is private. " Hanna was all business again.

"Ok. Dining room at 7 o'clock."

Chapter 15

Matt decided it was time to call Jonas. They all saw the corporate spaceplane dock, which could only mean brass had come up to put on the pressure. He had a short break, and took it to get back to the worker's quarters. He implemented Parm's ingenious patch and made the contact. Jonas immediately picked up.

Matt said, "Two minutes."

"Okay, I thought about what you said about the cheap components. Listen, there's nothing I can do-"

"Chicken shit…"

"No, wait, let me finish. What if I could get some of you on that flight to monitor the units? If there is a problem, one of you could fix it. That way, we stay on schedule, but put in a human check and balance."

Matt realized what Jonas was saying. He would have to leave Earth for good and become a colonist. But, it also meant that he could potentially saves countless lives.

"Well, you can count me in. How many were you thinking?"

"My calculations show we need four volunteers for the trip. Can you recruit? Ideally, when the formal ask goes out, you will support it on the worker side. We don't need any problems."

"I'll work this out from my end."

"Good."

"Hey, Jonas… Good job, buddy."

"Okay. Out," and the connection was lost.

Matt smiled inwardly. A small victory. Not a complete production change, but at least a solution. *Jonas, I knew that you weren't the heartless corporate bastard that some people think you are.*

Now, who would want to volunteer for this duty? He wanted Parm for sure. Sandy might be a bit harder – he knew how badly she wanted to go back home. How about that crazy Canadian? He was really skilled. He realized that he would have to tell more people about the problems, which made for the possibility of a tense situation on the floor. *This thing can't blow up in our face right now.*

Matt decided to ask Parm first and see what he thought. He headed down to the floor, grabbing one of his interface components on the way. He had to have some reason to talk to Parm, and it would make a good prop.

Parm was busy working to meet his quota and seemed a bit annoyed at the interruption. Speaking in a low voice, Matt quickly brought Parm up to speed.

"Count me in," Parm said. "My karma would be forever out of whack if I didn't do this."

Matt was surprised at Parm's quick response, but he was happy that he already had one recruit. "We need two more, but I'm worried about telling more people about the faulty units. Who can we trust?"

Parm shrugged. "Up to you. I keep to myself. I don't really know anyone that well."

"Okay, I'll think about it. In the meantime, keep this close to your chest. We don't need a riot up here."

Parm simply nodded and got back to work.

Chapter 16

Jonas was fidgeting while he waited for Hanna. She was fifteen minutes late. *Not that she's gonna stand me up. Where else can she go?*

Hanna came striding into the corporate dining room looking like a million bucks. Jonas stood as she approached, and went around to offer her a chair. She accepted and sat down, putting the white napkin on her lap.

The view was spectacular from the dining room. A fully panoramic view of the Earth below, only partially obscured by the huge spacedock.

"I hope everything is to your liking, Hanna?"

"Fine. Thanks. The rooms are small, but what do you expect being in orbit? That is quite the spectacular view."

"I never get tired of it. It's amazing to think that ten billion people live down there on top of each other. Up here it looks so peaceful and serene."

A discrete server came in with the first course, a lobster salad with balsamic vinaigrette dressing. The Sémillon wine perfectly complimented the starter dish. The corporate spaceplane had brought up some very high-end supplies, and Jonas had made sure that there was nothing but the best for Hanna.

Hanna picked up where the discussion left off. "Well, that is why this first colony ship is so important. The Earth is simply not big enough for all of humankind. We need to take to the stars now, before it's too late."

"Too late?"

"Jonas, it is inevitable that the humans of Earth will eventually destroy themselves. There are simply too many lingering hatreds. Look at 911-2. That is the tip of the iceberg. Do you think that's going to be the end of it? Sadly, I don't see it ending well for humanity."

"Well, that's a bit pessimistic. We've lasted for thousands of years and continue to thrive. We managed to get through the Black Death, two world wars, the Persian Gulf Wars, and the flu pandemic of 2049. Nature has a way of compensating."

"Well, perhaps you're right. Nonetheless, I don't believe that we should put all of our eggs in one basket, do you?"

"No, of course not. It's important that we reach out to the stars. I just think that my reasons for doing so are a bit different than yours."

The main course came. Rack of lamb, new potatoes, and asparagus. The wine was a rare Domaine de la Romanee-Conti La Tache Grand Cru Monopole from Cote de Nuits, France. Everything was exquisite.

After they had finished eating, Hanna asked, "Oh, and what are *your* reasons?"

"Reasons for what?"

"For our going into space."

"Oh, yes. Humans became the dominant species on Earth due to our self-awareness. No other species has our level of intelligence, but we also have a very strong survival instinct. We aren't an apex predator. We aren't the fastest, biggest, strongest, or even most prolific animals on the planet. But we create. We create science, art, music, literature. We're never satisfied with the status quo. We constantly challenge ourselves as a species to develop and grow. Leaving the planet is really the logical extension of this drive."

Hanna chuckled. "A philosopher. And I thought you were just a pretty face." Hanna gave Jonas a look that was just a little softer than she normally projected. Jonas responded exactly as she expected – she could see the blood rush to his cheeks.

"Well, arm chair philosopher, anyway. I actually did some studies in behavioral sciences in undergrad. That's the best part about first degrees, you can just learn what you want to and get inspired. The real career work comes in post-grad. My MBA was tough, but it got me a good job. And look where I am now." Jonas motioned around him, trying to deflect from his obvious discomfort. There were other tables, but he had ensured that the other corporate teams were all fed and out of the room before Hanna arrived.

Hanna reached out and put her hand on Jonas'. As she did the server came in with the dessert, and she quickly removed her hand and sat back as the crème brulée and fresh fruit were placed in front of them. Cognac Frapin Cuvee 1888 and espresso provided a triumphant finish. Jonas was very proud of himself.

"Jonas, I have to admit something to you. It is very difficult being a woman in this corporate world. It isn't fair, but we have to be that much tougher and smarter just to be on par with what is expected of you men. I can come across as a bit of a bitch, I know," Hanna said, tipping her head forward just a bit to show vulnerability.

"Not at all, Hanna. Strong women are extremely attractive. I have to admit that you can be a bit scary, but at the same time your confidence is like an aphrodisiac to me."

"So, I don't intimidate you?"

"Well, honestly a bit. But, I also respect you a great deal. You had to have worked your butt off to get where you are so fast."

"Yes, years of boarding school. University in Boston. Training in Switzerland. Eighty hour work weeks. It has been all business."

Jonas put his hand on her hand. "I sure wish that there wasn't a non-fraternization policy with the company."

Hanna looked up at Jonas and smiled. "Those rules don't apply to us."

Hanna stood, Cognac in hand, and gave Jonas eyes that would melt an ice cube. She moved towards her stateroom and Jonas followed, amazed at his incredible fortune.

Chapter 17

Dr. Little had used all of his enhanced intellect and pushed his team to the limit, but he believed that he had perfected the treatment. The patient was on the operating table in the induced comma. Gregory Hicks' apparition was once again looking down from the observation area. He could feel Hicks' eyes burning into the back of his head, even though he knew intellectually that the CEO was hundreds of miles away. Failure was not an option. Dr. Little injected the new nanobot configuration into the IV and waited. Nothing happened at first, which was normal. Then the patient's heart rate started to rise, as did his brain activity. *Come on, come on.* Just when the readings were getting to a critical level, they slammed back down to normal and the patient became stable. Dr. Little glanced up to the observation area and saw Hicks' holoprojection looking down frowning, but also nodding.

Dr. Little smiled inwardly. *I just made history.*

Chapter 18

Sandy was exhausted. The super was pushing her to the limit and she was barely making her quota. Normally she was well ahead of the pack in terms of production stats, but up top, the pressure was relentless. *It's a bloody sweatshop.*

Dirty, tired, hungry, and cranky, the last thing she needed was a room full of horny men hitting on her. She grabbed her rations and headed straight for her bunk. *At least the coffin has some privacy.* Sandy was so fixated on her goal of getting away from the rest of the crew that she literally ran into Matt in the bunk hall. Sandy blushed. She must look terrible.

Matt smiled. "Well, you look a sight," he said. Sandy was about to snap at him when he continued, "A sight for sore eyes, that is."

Sandy rolled her eyes and chuckled. "Where did you get that line, on a bubble gum wrapper?"

Matt pretended to be offended. "Hey, I was trying to be charming."

"You're a goof, Matt. I don't know why I put up with you. Listen, I'm going to try to eat in the-"

A siren cut her off, and a loud repeating warning announcement came on:

ARTIFICAL GRAVITY FAILURE IMMINENT

Within seconds, they went weightless and started to float. With that came the momentary feeling of their stomachs jumping. Sandy and Matt held arms and drifted in the hall as they adjusted to the zero g . Matt nodded up to her bunk and grinned. Sandy grinned back. They went up while all hell was breaking loose around them. A perfect time to break the no-fraternization rule.

After about thirty minutes of maneuvering and experimenting, they figured out a system. Afterward, they both had a bit of a giggle. Sandy whispered "Well, check that off the bucket list. Zero-g sex. Harder than I thought. Harder than a water-bed."

"At least we had the coffin ceiling. First time I was actually glad that these things are so tiny."

Matt was grinning ear to ear. He knew he only had moments, so he took the opportunity to talk. "Listen, I really hate to bring this up now, but there's something really important that you need to know." He told her about the construction issues and the solution that Jonas had come up with. He also told her that he and Parm were going to volunteer.

Sandy immediately clammed up. She pushed Matt away. "How dare you. Leading me on and then telling me that you're going away forever. Get out of my bunk."

Sandy gave Matt a big boot and he floated out of the bunk, stark naked. He just managed to get a handhold when the gravity came back. Everything fell to the floor, including Matt, his clothes tumbling down on top of him.

Matt quickly got dressed and climbed up to her third row bunk.

"Sandy, you don't understand. I want you on the crew too. I want you to come with us."

Sandy had her arms crossed and was clearly stewing. It didn't help that she was already near the end of her rope with the grueling work schedule. She wasn't thinking straight. Matt was asking her to come with him to the new colony? That would mean leaving Earth behind. She didn't have anyone back there, but it was home. It was terra firma. It was unnatural to be in space. People were meant to stand on the ground.

"Sandy, please understand. I don't trust anyone else. You're one of the best mechanics we have. People are going to die if we don't do this. Displaced are going to die. Do you get that?"

"Is that the only reason that you want me to come?" Sandy asked, getting angrier by the second.

Matt was confused by her anger, "Well, of course I want you to come because you, I mean we, I mean the two of us have a thing, right?"

"Matt, you are one of the dumbest smart guys I know." Sandy's temper was on a slow boil.

Matt's brow was screwed up tight as he contemplated this conversation. It was not going at all as he had planned. "Look, I'm not very good at this stuff. The thing is that I care about you a lot. I always have. I don't want you to be in danger, but I want you with me. I also know that we need you on this team. I don't know how to say this right."

Sandy looked hard at Matt, took a deep breath and unclenched her fists. "You are one confusing guy. I'll tell you what. If you don't take me, I will definitely have to throw you out an air lock."

Matt chuckled. "I have no doubt that you could do that." He was not only relieved that he had his third person, he was also really happy that it was Sandy. He had denied his real feelings for so long. He shook his head. *I can't get all mushy about this. I have to stay focused or we're all screwed.*

Chapter 19

Jonas was scrambling to find out how there was a malfunction in the artificial gravity on the manufacturing module. After some digging, it was determined that a micro-meteor had punctured one of the external gravity regulators, sending the entire system into flux. Of course, that meant that they would probably lose a day just trying to clean up the mess and get all of the work stations back to operational status. *Hanna is going to be pissed. But then again, I know how to make that better.*

For the last two weeks, Hanna had been a love machine. He had never had so much sex in his life, and it was the best he had ever had. Hanna was absolutely insatiable. Jonas decided to visit her in her state room.

"We need to end this now," Hanna said in a very matter of fact tone.

"You mean the artificial gravity failure? We have it under control, and we'll re-double our work schedule."

"No, not that. I have to go down below on the next shuttle. We can't have any lingering issues between us that might compromise the work."

Actually, Hanna had just confirmed that she was pregnant. She had timed the excursion perfectly while she was ovulating, and she had Jonas dialed in on the quota. Double mission accomplished.

"I don't know what to say. I was feeling pretty good about us."

"There is no us, Jonas. This was a fun fling and now it's done. My work schedule is far too busy for a long-term commitment. I hope that you understand."

Jonas was at a loss for words.

"The shuttle will arrive in an hour and I intend to be on it. Please make sure that all of my luggage and work materials are properly accounted for."

Hanna turned around in her chair and went back to work on her holoscreen. Jonas was clearly dismissed. He made his way to his office and just sat there in a daze. *What just happened?*

The announcement came ten days later. Volunteers were requested for maintenance crew on Colonial I during the space voyage. It was made obvious that this was a multi-year commitment, at a minimum, and that they may never return to Earth. Three names came in immediately. Surprisingly, there was also a fourth.

After a few more days an announcement was made that Matt, Sandy, Parm, and Carter Williams would be making the big journey to Mars. Now they just had to put their heads down and get to work. It would be pretty much the same old, same old until the launch.

Chapter 20

After six months, Hanna was ready to have the treatment introduced to her child. It was intriguing to her to think that the treatment could be extended in utero to an unborn child.

Dr. Little came and visited her in pre-op to explain the procedure. This time she would be awake during the procedure, and the gene-nanobot treatment would be introduced through an IV. The delivery system had been refined so that only one treatment was required.

Nurses wheeled Hanna into the OR, and they set up the monitors for herself and her unborn child. After Dr. Little was sure that everything was perfect, he asked Hanna if she was fine with him proceeding.

"Of course," she said with a smile.

Dr. Little introduced the treatment through the IV and they waited. He viewed the body scan machine that was able to track the progress of the gene therapy and nanobot throughout Hanna's body. As programmed, the smart machines were directed to the uterus and went to work on the baby boy.

As Dr. Little had perfected the therapy, he was not surprised when the treatment seemed to be a success.

"Now that the procedure has been completed, we need to induce labor. While the child is only six months into its development, we have sufficient premature birth systems on site to safely incubate the baby. We need to begin testing immediately to ensure that the Phase 2 protocol has no adverse side effects."

"Of course, Doctor Little, proceed."

A nurse added Pitocin to Hanna's IV and within a few minutes her labor started. As the birth progressed, Hanna's internal systems were able to compensate for the excruciating pain of labor. After a six hours, she was had dilated to ten centimeters, and the nurse told her to push.

At that precise moment, everything changed.

Emotions flooded into Hanna's brain: surprise, fear, disgust, anger, then a profound sadness, all within a few seconds. She realized that for the previous five years, ever since her gene-nanobot treatment, she had been a captive in her mind, viewing her own life in the third person. It was horrific. She screamed at the top of her lungs as she pushed her son into the world, but none of the cry was from the pain of the birth.

She could see that he was incredibly tiny. The nursing team cut the umbilical chord and rushed the premature child off in an incubator. She was left alone with a nurse to help with the after-birth and to get her stitched up. Hanna had experienced some tearing.

She lay in the maternity bed with new, crazy thoughts rushing through her head, and at the same time felt the emotions of having her child suddenly taken away from her. She shut her eyes and concentrated on getting under control. She knew she was on the verge of a complete meltdown.

Hanna wasn't sure what had happened, but she was convinced that she was now exposed to grave danger.

After Hanna had been cleaned and settled, Dr. Little and Gregory Kicks both walked in.

"Well, how is my favorite executive?" Gregory Hicks asked.

"Just fine, sir. I believe that the procedure was a perfect success."

"Very good."

Dr. Little said, "I agree. We will continue to monitor the child now that he is outside of the womb. He will be a great test subject for our Phase 2 study."

Hanna's heart started to beat faster, and she had to use all of her willpower not to react. "Of course, whatever is best for the Company."

"Good girl," Hicks said. "Well, I'm off. As soon as you're up and ready, I need you up top again to supervise the final phase of the colonial ship construction."

"Yes, sir. I will get up top as soon as possible."

Hicks nodded and left, Doctor Little following on his heels. They left Hanna quite alone, and feeling scared for the first time in years.

Chapter 21

Jonas shivered with déjà vu as the XTC-Mark II docked. Hanna was on that ship. He had no idea how to act around her. He knew he had to keep things professional, but he was full of anger and bitterness at how she had treated him six months earlier.

The 2063 optimum launch window for Mars was fast approaching, and the colonists were starting to be transported up and placed into hibernation. Most of the colonists would be in stasis for at least a year, if not more – getting to Mars was only the first step. The next step was to slowly integrate the colonists into the massive domed living environments. The ship would stay in orbit until the next window opened, and then it would return to Earth in order to start the process all over again, slowly growing the colony over a number of decades.

Hanna arrived and walked in with her head held high, the same hyper-intelligent look on her face. Jonas couldn't help himself - his heart skipped a beat when he saw her, and he could feel the heat in his face. He was upset with himself for reacting this way; he had been determined not to respond.

"Jonas. It's been a while. Walk me to my quarters, please."

"Of course, Ms. Smith." Jonas signaled to an assistant to bring Hanna's bags.

Once inside her room, Hanna pulled out an electronic device that Jonas had never seen before. She twisted it and a red light came on.

"This is a scrambler. I don't have a lot of time before the system notices and automatically compensates. Jonas, I'm so sorry for the way I treated you. I was on a mission and I used you. I don't have time to explain, but the mission to Mars is not what it seems. Can I count on you to help me?"

Jonas was absolutely stunned. Again. This woman never ceased to amaze and confuse. "Of course. Whatever you need."

Clearly relieved, Hanna turned off the scrambler and immediately started ordering Jonas around. He played along and acted the obsequious fool, knowing in his heart that he actually had a chance with her. That was as big a motivator as he could need.

Chapter 22

After the birth of her son, Hanna had been worried that the shut-off nanobots would reassert themselves and she would be under their control again. As it turned out, the side-effect from the in utero treatment of her child was permanent. She couldn't explain it, but she wasn't about to complain. Hanna had written herself a warning, but had then destroyed it. If she turned back, she knew that she would choose to reveal the side-effect to the research team. She considered attempting escape, but if she was caught she would be forced to explain herself. She had decided to take her chances.

Hanna had been left to grieve alone. No one had given her any support; none should have been necessary. She was enhanced and all of her emotions were controlled. She had to concentrate very hard to maintain the emotional detachment that had been required of her.

She had vowed to herself that she would rescue her son. She just needed time and space to figure out a strategy. First, she had to figure out what was going on. She had always been on a "need to know" basis working with Gregory Hicks. He was clearly the key to all of this. She needed to recover physically from her labor. As she recuperated, Hanna had used her enhanced intellect to create a plan.

Now, she sat in her stateroom in the spacedock and planned her next move.

Chapter 23

Gregory Hicks sat in the boardroom with four other CEOs, two men and two women. The room was completely soundproof, and no electronic device could penetrate the security nets. This was one of the only places on Earth where these five people could speak freely in person. The Chair rotated, and it was Gregory's turn to run the meeting.

"I would like to call this meeting to order." The motion was made, seconded, and voted on in the affirmative. Strict adherence to Robert's Rules of Order was always maintained. This was the Company way.

Hicks reported, "Next item on the agenda is the Mars mission. At this time I would like to report that all systems are go for the scheduled launch January 2, 2063. Colonists are now being transported and placed into hibernation. Mars Colonial Base 1 is near completion."

A tall, severe looking grey-haired woman queried, "And what of the nanobot treatments? I hear that there had been some delays. We can't be having an unruly mob in the colonies, now can we."

"I assure you, Candice, we have that fully under control," Hicks said. "Our research team, under Dr. Little, has perfected the nanobot treatment. The hibernation period is the perfect time to introduce the nanobots to the colonists. When they awaken, they will be very compliant workers. You will also be very happy to know that we have introduced a special variant that allows us to hit a kill switch. If there are any problems with individuals, or even crops of workers, we can simply switch them off and try again. Of course, we cannot have automatons. We need to give the workers the impression that they have free will, but in fact we can control responses via server connectivity. These little machines are really quite ingenious."

Across the table, Hans Gruberman spoke up. "And we are all in agreement that the longevity gene therapy shall continue to be for a select few? The workers will probably live longer due to the reparative properties of the treatment, but the aging gene will still be turned on?"

A quite striking blonde woman in her mid-forties added, "Yes, I believe that is the consensus. While it may be advantageous to have colonists live for centuries, we will have population control issues. Also, we do not know about the long term effects of the treatment. We may find over time that the nanobots lose their efficacy. Keeping life spans manageable makes the most sense."

Gregory nodded. "Then I would like someone to put forward the motion that the Mars Mission proceed as planned, with workers receiving only the nanobot treatment." The motion was proposed, seconded, and voted in the affirmative.

"Next on the agenda is Kepler-62e. Although this planet is twelve hundred light years away, time is less of an issue for the Company now that we plan to be around for many years to come. I suggest that we consider ramping up research on interstellar propulsion systems. Colonization of Kepler-62e and other planets of this type has always been the long term goal of the Company." Gregory put up the time-line and cost projections for the Kepler-62e project on floating holoscreens. The numbers were staggering, but not one of the board members flinched. Gregory continued as more charts and graphs appeared. "The Mars colony revenue projections over the next one hundred years are sufficient to cover the colonial expansion project."

The fifth board member, a quiet Chinese gentleman, finally spoke. "We now plan in centuries, not decades. This is truly the next step for mankind. We have no time for evolution to take its course, we have caused the next Great Leap forward. We are in control of our destiny, not random mutations. We have become gods of our own creation."

All of the board nodded with approval. Yes, they had fooled nature itself, and ensured that humankind would not become extinct like every other species.

"Yes, well said, Li Wei. Well said. Can we have a motion to approve the proposed Kepler-62e proposal?" Motion, seconded and approved.

"Next on the agenda, review of our ongoing world events action plan. Of course, 911-2 resulted in exactly what we wanted: final control of North America through the military and Homeland Security, and a huge mobile workforce. And of course, a willing group of colonists. The so-called Displaced have become the army of worker drones that we always envisioned. I have to congratulate you once again Li Wei for a masterful plan…"

Chapter 24

Hanna had thought long and hard about how she had managed to gain control of her mind again. Like the common reed frog that can change sex when there are not enough males to procreate, nature had figured out ways to compensate for crises in a species. In humans, the female maternal instinct was incredibly strong, in many ways helping to evolve the species. Giving birth to her son must have triggered hormonal responses that effected parts of her brain. Hanna figured that humans really only played at being God. In the end, natural systems were simply too complex to fully comprehend. It was that very complexity that had brought her back, and she aimed to keep it that way.

She had been very careful since being freed to act exactly as she had before. That meant walking away from her child and carrying on the work of the Company, as distasteful as that was, but she realized that this was a long game. She was fortunate to have received the gene therapy as well as the nanobot treatments. She was amongst a select group of young executives who had been groomed to be the future corporate elite of an expanding universe. While the senior executives of the Company planned to stay on Earth, the highly controlled but brilliant young executives would become the Company representatives on each space colony. That was her destiny; at least that was what the Company had planned for her.

She knew that she could not do this alone, so her first priority was getting Jonas up to speed. She felt that she could trust him; if she was wrong, they were both as good as dead. The Company wouldn't hesitate to switch her off and throw Jonas out the nearest air lock.

Of course, eyes were everywhere. George Orwell could not have envisioned how deep the Big Brother hole could go. Surveillance was ubiquitous. Most people knew in their hearts that public spaces were littered with cameras, sensors, and tracking devices, but they chose simply to go about their lives as if they had anonymity. Some people saw this surveillance as a good thing: catch the criminals, make the cities safer for decent folk. The truth was that every person had a file on the grid, and each file was constantly cycled through an algorithm that calculated each person's life in such a way that every facet could be predicted. Any deviation from that path would immediately throw up a red flag, and the person would simply be visited by DHS and vanish. Some returned. Some didn't. As with most things in life, people turned a blind eye. As long as they had their holovision sports and toys, they were happy. Fear and consumerism: the American way. And that ideal had become the model for the world. Everyone craved what Americans had, even if they hated them.

Hanna's specialized implants and treatment gave her an advantage. She was in many ways a walking computer, so she was able to work on complex problems while still maintaining an outwardly human appearance. She could now feel the data input from an external source, and had the newfound ability to choose whether to act on it or not. She was worried that the data that she worked on in her brain could be automatically uploaded to the Central Command center, but she felt that was unlikely. As long as she was careful to act on the commands that were fed to her, she was not in immediate danger of discovery.

The next step was to figure out how to communicate with Jonas without tripping any alarms. Her brain went into overdrive working on this problem.

Hanna accessed some deep memories from her adolescence. Her academy instructors had given her a history of spy craft. During all wars, protection of intelligence around troop movements and offensive plans was paramount. During WW2 elaborate codes were created, including the infamous Enigma Machine used by the Nazis. In the Cold War that followed WW2, spies would often use newspaper classifieds and obituaries to communicate sensitive missives. Hanna needed to develop an unbreakable codec so that she could communicate with Jonas. She worked on this problem for a number of days, then drafted a series of "progress reports" to be presented to Jonas using the codec. She realized that she had to risk using the jammer one more time, even though it might trigger a warning of some kind.

With her heart pounding, Hanna made her way to Jonas' office with the scrambler and a micro-drive in her pocket. She would have very little time to convey her complex yet elegant codec to Jonas. She hoped that he would understand how to use it.

Hanna entered and sat down unannounced. "I have a report from head office that you need to read immediately."

"Hanna, I'm under the gun here. We're getting close to our launch window and there's a lot that needs to be done."

"You will find this relevant to your work." With that she hit the scrambler. "Listen, there isn't a lot of time." She quickly handed Jonas the drive and explained the code he would need to use to read the files on it. Then she turned the scrambler off.

"Well, if you insist. I really do have a lot to do," he said with a subtle nod.

Hanna got up and showed herself out. Short, sweet. In, out. She let out a breath, smoothed her skirt, and made her way back to her state room.

As she was walking back, her eyephone started to beep. She tapped and Gregory Hicks immediately came on.

"Hanna, is everything okay up there? We got some interference with the feed."

"Everything is fine, sir. We've been experiencing solar flare activity, and that can sometimes interfere with transmissions."

"Very good. Well, how are things going up there?"

"We are still a go for Mars launch. The colonists are being processed, and we have about fifty-two percent in hibernation. Treatment packages have also been activated and we expect full success."

"That's what I want to hear. You are turning out to be quite the asset to the Company, Hanna."

"Thank you, sir." She decided to take the opportunity. "Sir, I have a request. Mr. Harris has shown great promise. I would like to recommend him for a promotion, and possible treatment upgrade. I see him being the best candidate to oversee the colony integration."

"Yes, Hanna. He is certainly on the short list for that position." Gregory smirked. "Or is there another reason that you see him coming along? You two had quite a thing going on that assignment six months ago."

Hanna stayed deadpan. "As you know, Gregory, unlike you I do not suffer the annoying emotional issues facing most people. I am simply stating my recommendation."

Gregory chuckled again. "Well, you keep telling yourself that. I think you have a thing for that young man."

Hanna decided that she should take another tack. "Well, sir, he is rather physically appealing."

"Okay, well, consider him a bonus for all your hard work. I'll assign you to oversee the mission, traveling with the colonists. Bring Jonas along. You are authorized to add the gene package along with his nanobot treatment. He can do some good work – and be your personal plaything."

"Very good sir. It is an honor to serve the Company."

Gregory signed off.

Now Hanna had to break the news to Jonas.
He wasn't going home.

Chapter 25

Matt decided that it was time to check in on Jonas and make sure everything was on track. Now that the plan was out in the open, communication had gotten easier. Jonas had taken a 'personal interest' in the matter, which surprised but pleased Matt's supers; it gave them a chance to suck up to the boss. Jonas had assured him that the four mechanics were going to be added to the system in such a way that even the slightest problem with the hibernation units would trigger one of them to wake. They would be on a waking rotation, and if one of them became overwhelmed they would have the override authority to wake as many of the other three as was necessary.

The protocol was still to go through a super, not upper-management, so Matt and Jonas still couldn't communicate directly, but they had Parm's work around.

Jonas was anxious when Matt finally got through. "We have to meet right away. I can't talk about it here, but it involves the hibernation units. I'll get to you shortly." Jonas logged off abruptly.

What was Jonas on about? They had figured out the problem. They had a plan. Their people were safe. All that Matt could do was continue to work and wait.

The next day, Jonas called a meeting of the four mechanics who had volunteered for the mission. As a gesture of good will, he was inviting them all for a special dinner in the company dining room. Word got around the floor quickly. Whispers of *the last supper* and *oo, aren't they special* whipped around the work stations.

Matt did his very best to clean up, but it was difficult in the worker's area. He didn't have to worry, though. When they got over to the other side of the dock, they were ushered into a special cleansing unit, where months of grime were washed away. It was bliss. Their work clothes were left at the airlock and they were given plain but elegant garments for the occasion.

Jonas greeted them and ushered Matt, Parm, Sandy, and Carter into the dining area. It was utterly incredible to witness. The view of the Earth and the station was breathtaking. They all just stood there with their mouths open.

"Come, please sit down. We are very pleased that the four of you volunteered for this mission. It is the least that we can do to honor you with a good meal." With that, the server came around with champagne flutes followed by hors d'oeuvres.

Jonas and Hanna had gone to a great deal of trouble to ensure that there would be a period of time when surveillance would go down. After Jonas had read the deciphered report he had been in utter disbelief, but eventually it started to make sense. The utter lack of regard for human life, the unregulated technology that was being implemented into this mission, and just the way that people like Hanna had acted. It was like a new species of human had been created, one that acted more like an apex predator than a civil, moral person. Since then, Jonas had used the same codec to send "reports" back to Hanna. He was certainly not as good at it and his reports were oddly worded, but she managed to figure them out. After Jonas had told her of his relationship with Matt, and how they had figured out the hibernation-unit problem, they both agreed that the maintenance volunteers had to be brought in.

The main course of steak, potatoes, carrots, and broccoli had arrived. Matt hadn't had real food in so long, he was having a hard time keeping it in. He could see that his colleagues were not fairing any better. The steak melted in his mouth. He closed his eyes and tried to remember every bite and every swallow.

Jonas realized that this was nearly cruel of him, but he had to meet somewhere he had control. He checked his eyephone time monitor often. Hanna was going to make the system go down across the ship at precisely 20:32 pm.

The desert came and the volunteers all seemed to be in ecstasy. Jonas dismissed the server.

As the clock turned over, the lights flickered slightly, signaling that the system was down. Jonas didn't waste any time. "Listen up, we don't have a lot of time. What I'm going to say may seem farfetched, but it's true and you need to listen carefully." Jonas had their entire attention.

"The company that's behind the mining colony mission has developed a nanobot technology that not only regulates physical human systems, but can also be used to control people's brain function. They've figured out a way to literally override a person's free will. We know this because Hanna was under their control and somehow managed to break free from the system. Hanna's secret hasn't been discovered by the Company, so she's managed to find out that the colonists are receiving the therapy when they receive their hibernation drugs for the trip to Mars. When they arrive, they will all be completely compliant workers; the beginning of the Company's long-term colonization plan. People relegated to worker bees."

All sound had stopped in the dining room; you could have heard a pin drop. Each of the diners had looks of shock and incredulity on their faces. It was a moment that they would remember for their entire lives.

Carter was the first to speak. "Jesus H. Christ! You all know what this is! It's the logical extension of multi-national corporate greed! In Canada, our natural resources were all sold off to the highest bidder. Chinese, European, and American interests raped our land and polluted our waters with trucks, trains, pipelines, freighters. The final straw was when they started piping out our fresh water with the same pipes they'd used for oil. After 911-2 we became second-class citizens in North America. We traded security for freedom. Well, I'm sick of being polite. I signed up for the Mars maintenance gig out of despair, but this gives me hope. Whatever you need, I'm in." Carter set his jaw with determination.

Matt didn't know what to say. He had new respect for Carter. He looked at Sandy and Parm, who obviously felt the same way, then over at Jonas. "How much time do we have?"

"Maybe only a few more minutes. Know that Hanna and I will be coming on the trip to Mars with you. We're going to make sure that you're not affected by the nanobot treatment. We aren't sure how yet, but you can count on us for that. "

"I may be able to help with that," Parm said. "I'm in charge of final inspections and delivery systems. I had always wondered about the need for so many components to the hibernation system. I believe that I can figure out which system delivers that treatment and deactivate it for all of us."

"Good, Parm. See if you can make that happen. Only the four of you and me, we can't deactivate all of the units because that would cause suspicion. In the meantime, not a word to anyone. If word gets out about what's about to happen, we'll have a riot on our hands. That can only result in liquidation of all of the workers, including yourselves. We'll be in touch."

With no time to spare, the lights flickered again. Jonas started laughing and all of the guest followed his cue and laughed along. Sandy launched into a joke. "So this guy goes into a bar. He does a shot, opens his wallet, and looks at it. Then he does the whole thing again. After a few times, the bartender asks what he's doing. The man says that after each drink he looks at a picture of his wife in his wallet. When she starts looking good, he knows it's time to head home." They all groaned, and Parm slapped Carter on the back. After a few more chuckles, they headed back to the crew quarters.

Jonas was sad to see his old chum head back. He missed the easy camaraderie that he always shared with Matt. He was really the only person he could truly act like himself around.

At least he had Hanna. What an amazing and courageous woman. He was definitely boxing above his weight, but... *Who knows, maybe I have a chance with her.*

Hanna's plan to bring the surveillance systems down was nothing short of brilliant. Creating an energy surge in the server room had caused an automatic system shutdown and re-boot. She used the server's own safety and diagnostics against itself. The surge could be attributed to a number of space-related issues; they were always dealing with radiation issues. It would keep the techs scratching their heads for months.

One last thing that Jonas had been dreading. How was he going to break the news of his imminent departure to his Mom, Dad, and sister? *Hey, see ya later, going to be gone for a few years and maybe forever.*

Part III The Journey

Hanna Smith represented the cutting edge of cybernetics; not the sci-fi horror movie version, with metal parts roughly stitched to the skin of the poor cyborg. No, Hanna represented the enhancement of humans through implants, genetics, and nano-computer technology. Simply put, Hanna was human being 2.0. She could directly interface with any server and process this information at lightning speeds. Sensors in her brain allowed her to maintain optimum efficiency at all times. Primitive triggers such as fight-and-flight response were controlled to ensure that Hanna always stayed calm, cool, and collected in any situation. Emotions such as hate, love, fear, were all tempered by the millions of nanobots that swam through her system. The Company had thought that they had created the perfect executive, compliant and completely devoted to the profitability of the Company. That was until she broke free of from her bonds. Then she became the Company's most feared adversary.
- Cassandra Taylor, chief colonial historian

Chapter 1

Matt lay in the hiberchamber. His heart was beating very fast, his anxiety level through the roof. *Oh, why didn't I choose the blue pill? Ignorance is bliss. Parm better have got this right.* As the technicians hovered over his chamber making last minute adjustments, Matt slowly started drifting off. Everything went black.

Suddenly he was awake, alarms were going off, and a warning announcement was repeating:

HIBERCHAMBER FAILURE IMMINENT UNIT 837

Matt froze. Was he the same person? Had the nanobots turned him into a corporate slave? He didn't feel any different. Incredibly groggy, but the same. Matt untangled himself from the chamber and tried to get his bearings. They should have warned him that coming out was like having the worst hang-over he had ever had. *Suck it up, buttercup.*

Matt staggered down the rows of hiberchambers and thanked the lord that artificial gravity was considered an important part of space travel. Obviously it wasn't important for the hibernating colonists, but long-term weightlessness on such a voyage would create serious health problems for the flight crew, even with all the advances in space medicine.

Murphy's Law. The faulty chamber had to be the farthest way, didn't it. Matt finally arrived at unit 837. Just as Parm had said, the regulator component was acting up. If it continued to give the hibernation drugs at this rate, the person would never come out of deep sleep. Matt went back to the workbay and got his tools and a new regulator unit from storage. After about forty-five minutes he had successfully replaced the part.

With the crisis solved, Matt decided to check out the ship. He headed to the flight deck, where a rotating skeleton crew ensured that the ship stayed on course. Really it was on autopilot, but you never know. At the entrance to the flight deck Matt tapped the intercom and announced who he was. A scanner activated, and then he heard a click.

The heavy blast door slid open and Matt stepped through and took a quick look around. Straight ahead was a spectacular view of space. With the ship rotating to provide gravity, the visual would have been nauseating, but instead of showing the spin, the view was set at one plane of view that was refreshed every spin. The flight controls and pilot seats were set back from the windows to allow space for the holoprojector, which was constantly displaying telemetry, fuel, and other things that Matt could only guess at. The entire front of the space craft was set up to house and provide for the crew. There was a common area, a kitchen, and entrances to what Matt assumed were living quarters. At a table by the kitchen Matt found two men playing cards. One had the insignia of a Commander and the other a Lieutenant.

"Hey, looks exciting."

"So, you fixed the problem in cargo. Great, thought I might have to come down, not that I could do anything about it," the Commander said nonchalantly.

"Everything is under control, sir. So, where are we?"

"About forty five days in," the Lieutenant piped up. "We didn't expect any malfunctions so soon."

"Corporate let a bunch of marginal passes through the system. We expect to be busy."

The Commander finally looked up from his cards. "Commander Hoggs, and this is my navigator Lieutenant Jones."

"Matt, sir. Good to meet you. Mind if I grab a coffee and some grub?"

"Sure, but then you're going to have to go back under. We have limited supplies and a lot of days left. Especially if we're going to have that bloody alarm going off all the time."

Matt went into the galley and got some coffee and what could pass as food from the regulated dispenser. After finished he said, "Deal me in."

Chapter 2

Sandy gagged and felt like she was dying. Alarms were going off and the bloody announcement kept endlessly repeating. This was her sixth awakening, and it seemed to get more difficult every time. After the second failure she had created a little pre-failure kit and set it up beside her hiberchamber on a cart. She had three of the possible components that might fail and the tools to fix them. Before her last hibernation, she had taken the time to set up similar rigs at each of the other mechanic hiberchambers. Maybe they would like her idea.

Sandy dragged her ass out of the chamber and started wheeling the cart down the long corridor.

HIBERCHAMBER FAILURE IMMINENT UNIT 201

OK, I'm coming. Shut up already.

When Sandy got there she sighed. *Another circuit board. I swear these were designed to fail. Works fine in holoscreens. Those become obsolete as soon as they're delivered. Not so good in a life preserving hibernation chamber.*

She had this down to a science now, but the circuit board was the most involved procedure. It was placed in what had to be the most inopportune place to get to. She would have to talk to Parm about that part of the design. She was cursing his name right about now. *How many times can I do this? Time to talk to the Commander.*

She shuffled down to the flight deck and went through the security screen. This time the Commander was not on deck, it was the ranking Captain. Sandy groaned inwardly. The Captain could be a bit of a she-bitch.

"You look like shit."

"Thanks, Captain Johnson. I appreciate the observation."

"You aren't the only one who has to deal with this crap." The Captain nodded over towards Lieutenant Paca, who was busy under his navigation desk. Lucky for him, the Filipino navigator was small. Sandy wouldn't have wanted to work in that tight space.

"So where are we now, Captain?"

"We're a hundred and eighty days out, so about one-twenty to go."

Sandy put her head in her hands. There was no way that she could keep this up. Looking up, Sandy said, "Listen, Captain. Have you noticed that the number of chamber failures are on the rise? Hibernation wasn't designed for constant going under and waking up."

"What do you suggest? We don't have enough rations for the flight crew and the maintenance crew."

The team had anticipated this possibility and had made some provisions. One of the storage containers contained emergency food and water supplies. If they were very careful, they could survive the remainder of this trip. The container also contained portable cots, blankets, wet cleaning napkins, and most importantly a portable human waste recycling unit.

"Captain, our team was ready for this. We have some supplies. We can survive with what we have."

The Captain contemplated the request. "I have been concerned with the failure rates of the chambers. Listen, the colonists are your problem. My job is to get this tub into Mars orbit and get it back to Earth for the next trip. Don't make me come down there and flog you. Take it as a tentative yes."

"Thanks Captain. Mind if I clean up? Then I'll get out of your hair."

The Captain just grunted and turned back to her flight station. *I guess that conversation is over.*

The cleansing unit was glorious. With her head clear, she decided to make an executive decision. She had the overrides to awaken the others in the team, but there was something she had to do first. With a little smile on her face, she headed for the hiberchambers.

Chapter 3

"Mother fucker. Are you freakin' kidding me!"
Matt was not amused at being woken up. He
suddenly became very still – something was
wrong. It took him a second to figure it out –
there was no alarm. *What's going on?* His head
was pounding, and he felt like a train wreck.
When he opened his eyes he saw a blurred
vision. It looked like an angel.

"Hey handsome. Wakie, wakie, eggs and
bacie."

It was Sandy smiling down on him. She really
was a sight for sore eyes. Literally.

"Hey, baby."

Sandy helped Matt sit up. This was Matt's
seventh awakening and it was hitting him
hard. "Let's get you cleaned up."

Sandy led him to the mechanical room. She
had created a makeshift nest and set out some
food and water, as well as having raided the
nurses' station for some towels. She gave Matt
a hand bath, which he clearly appreciated. She
had also grabbed some painkillers and

electrolyte drink bottles. After Matt has taken his meds and gotten some food and liquids into him, Sandy decided it was time to have a chat.

"So, Matt. This is where we are. We are at day one eighty and have a hundred and twenty to go. We obviously can't keep this awakening schedule up. It's going to kill us. The Captain has agreed that we can fend for ourselves. I've done an inventory and if we're very careful, we should be able to stay awake until we get into Mars orbit. The question is when do we wake the rest of the team?"

Matt was still getting his bearings, and it took him a moment to think it through. "Have you figured out when we can safely wake the rest of the team? We need to put our heads together before we get there."

"I crunched the math. Looks like it's just you and me for next sixty days." Sandy smiled and wrapped her arms around Matt's neck. Matt leaned his head forward and touched her forehead to his. He seemed happy.

Chapter 4

Matt lay in their little cocoon, Sandy snuggled up to him, listening to the hum of the ship. They had had seven more failures in the past three weeks, for a total of thirty one. At this rate they would run out of some component replacements. Matt still had a hard time accepting that Worldstar would have actually knowingly allowed faulty units on board. Jonas had said something about "acceptable losses," but surely even looking at it coldly, losing colonists was not an efficient use of resources? Then Matt thought about the nanobots and the fact that this "Company" had created a way to actually control an entire human population. It was mind bending. A company ruling over people.

Matt thought back to before they left the spacedock. One of the biggest impediments to planning a strategy was being able to meet without being recorded by surveillance cameras and microphones. For days, the small team made notes of every surveillance device that they could see. They used old-school pen and paper to pass diagrams and notes to each other during meal times. Parm then calculated where the likely dead spots were. Storage areas were the best bet, but cameras would see them coming and going, which might have raised alarms; management was always paranoid about possible union organizing. Hiding in plain sight was another option, simply relying on the noise of the common area to mask their conversations, but Matt had felt that was too risky. In the end, it was Carter who had found their secret meeting place. Carter had done some electrical repair work on the space dock and was aware of a small maintenance area near the toilets. Parm confirmed that there was indeed a surveillance dead spot that would allow them all access to that panel. No one would question their comings and goings; basic human needs and all.

The maintenance area was tight, but they could all fit in. Matt recalled the detailed planning meetings, but for some reason another conversation came to the front of his mind.

"You think that this is all new? Companies ruling over people? My ancestors were subject to British colonization for hundreds of years. The worst part was that it was the East Indian Company that actually ruled for much of that time. That same company used India as a base for their massive Opium trade. That same company was involved in the African slave trade, along with another British Company called the Royal African," Parm said.

Carter, who had a new sense of purpose after finding out what was going on, had pointed out that things hadn't really changed at all. "Look at the great oil companies. Why do you think the USA went to war so many times in the Persian Gulf? Same deal as the East India Company, to protect American financial interests." While people had suffered mass genocides in Rwanda, Bosnia, and then Burma, nothing had been done until it was too late. There was no reason to go into those countries. It wasn't profitable.

Matt thought about those old slave ships that had traveled to the New World. They had transported people like cattle, and many had died on the journey. When people became commodities, they were treated like them. He thought of all of the Displaced in their hiberchambers and realized that there really was no difference. With all of the supposed progress that humankind had made, they were still capable of the most inhuman behavior.

Now with the nanobots and computerization, exploitation had become a science.

At another meeting Parm had gotten up the nerve to tell them even more good news. The hiberchamber design had a built-in system in the case of the unfortunate death of a colonist. Parm had been part of the original design team and they had discussed this very issue. In space, they couldn't leave a rotting carcass contaminating the area where the chambers sat in the hold. If a passenger died en-route, a chemical embalming fluid would be pumped into their body; they would basically be pickled. At the time, he had intellectually seen the logic in this, but with the failures of the units being an inevitability, Parm was ashamed that he had helped in that system design.

Matt's sordid reveries were interrupted with another alarm. Sandy jumped up like a rabbit and started to get her things together, half asleep. Matt put a hand on her arm.

"Slow down, sweetheart. We'll get there in time."

HIBERCHAMBER FAILURE IMMINENT
UNIT 643

Matt and Sandy wheeled the maintenance cart down the long corridor. When they reached the faulty unit, they saw that it was a simple regulator issue. *Thank God, a quickie.*

After they were safely back in their nest, Sandy said, "You know, we're going to run out of components. We brought every spare part we had in stock, but if things progress the way that they are, we're going to be in trouble."

"I was thinking about that. I wish we could just wake some of them up, but all of the supplies are in orbit around Mars with the advance supply ship. They either die in their chamber or they die of starvation. I think I would choose the former."

"I think that we have to wake up the team, Matt, including Jonas and Hanna. We have to figure this problem out."

"Do we have enough supplies?"

"We've been very good so far. If we're brutal with the rations, we can all make it."

"Good thing that we got override codes for everyone. Okay, let's get 'er done."

Chapter 5

Hanna came slowly out of her deep sleep. She lay still as the computer disengaged the apparatus and the nanobots in her system quickly compensated for any discomfort she felt. The data stream told her that they were presently on course and about ninety days away from Mars orbit. Hanna opened her eyes and saw Matt and Sandy standing next to her chamber. Judging by their hair growth, it looked like they had been out of their sleep for some time. Hanna sat up and hung her legs over the table. Matt and Sandy were looking at her in a peculiar way.

"Hi, you two. What's up?"

Sandy said incredulously, "So no blinding headaches, blurry vision, or nausea?"

"The nanobots have compensated for all that. I am one hundred percent functional and ready to go."

"You are freakin' kidding me," Matt said.

"No, I'm freakin' not, Matt," Hanna said back with a grin. "So why the early awakening? What's going on?"

"We have a problem, and we think we should wake the team up," Sandy said.

Matt went on, "We've already had thirty-two failures, and the rate of problem units seems to be escalating. We're going to run out of parts if this keeps up."

Sandy finished Matt's thought. "And, we can't wake them up, because we don't have enough supplies. All the food and water that we need is in orbit around Mars in the advance supply ship."

Hanna had a good look at Matt and Sandy and smiled inwardly. *Finishing each other's sentences. Like an old married couple.*

"Even if we wanted to awaken some of the colonists, we don't have the override codes for that. Only the Captain has those, and she's not about to use them. Theoretically, I could use my level of access to get those codes like I did for Jonas and me, but doing that for the hibernating colonists would expose us for sure. We simply can't chance that."

"So the only way is to wait until people are at risk. That truly sucks," Matt said in frustration.

Hanna got up and Matt and Sandy showed her to their little bungalow in the storage room.

"Cozy. Too bad that there are no sleeping quarters back here. I guess there was never any plan for conscious people," Hanna said with an ironic overtone. "I am famished."

"We have to go easy with rations. That's part of what we need to discuss," Sandy said as she prepared an allotment of food and water for Hanna.

Hanna had become used to a pretty high standard of living, so this slop looked like something only hogs would eat, but her hunger overwhelmed her revulsion. "Yummy." Hanna tasted a spoon of one of the different colored pastes. *Tastes just like it looks.*

While she was eating, Matt brought her to up to speed with their issues. She was also getting a feed of priority ship functions through the ship data-stream. As a high-ranking executive, she had top-level clearance. In fact, her clearance was higher than even the Captain's. Obviously her awakening would find its way back to Earth's grid, and a call was inevitable. In the meantime, Hanna had to concentrate on the problem at hand.

"So, let me get this straight. We expect more failures than we have parts for, but if we wake more than our team, we won't have enough supplies to keep them alive. Is that about right?"

"In a nutshell, yes," said Sandy, deep in thought.

"The big issue is water," Hanna continued. "People can theoretically survive for a long time, weeks without food, but water is the most important thing. I'm assuming that you considered this?"

"We have. We were hoping you can access the system to see what water supplies there are," Matt said.

"Already done. The flight crew is fairly self-contained. They started with roughly one hundred and fifty percent of their food needs and a recycling waste system that only requires a small amount of new water to stay operational essentially indefinitely. It is possible that a small number of people could use that system, but anything over two or three new people would overtax the recycling unit very quickly. It is unlikely that the Captain would allow even that if it were you or Sandy, but she couldn't refuse Jonas and myself."

"Well, that settles that. You and Jonas will have to muscle your way up front. The question is whether we need the entire team?" Sandy asked.

"Well I for one want Parm. We're going to need his brains for sure. Carter would be helpful, but for now, we may want to let him stay in hibernation," Matt said.

"I agree, let's wake Jonas and Parm," Hanna said.

Chapter 6

Hanna stood over Jonas' hiberchamber. Even though she had received the executive treatment package for Jonas, including the life extending gene therapy, she couldn't let him use it yet. She could extend Jonas' life, but with the introduction of the required nanobots he would become subject to manipulation from Central control. He would betray them without even thinking about it, and feel like he was making the choice with his own free will. It would seem obvious to him that he was making the right decision in exposing their team of rebels. She shuddered when she thought back to how she had been. No, she would have to wait until she was sure that Jonas would not ever be under the control of the system.

Matt entered the override code. The unit automatically dispensed the required chemicals and woke Jonas, who went through the expected painful awakening ritual. Finally, he spoke up. "I promise that I will never drink again."

Matt laughed. "I've heard that one before, buddy."

Hanna put a hand on Jonas' arm. "Hey, handsome."

"Hey. So what's the occasion?"

"We need to get the team up," Sandy explained. "We're reaching a critical level of unit failures and we need to figure out how to deal with the situation."

"Okay, give me a minute to get my bearings. I could use some grub."

Matt chuckled. "Oh, we have grub… juicy steak, potatoes, fine wine…"

"Yeah, yeah. I know, I had that one coming."

Hanna and Matt helped Jonas up, and they made their way back to the storeroom. After Jonas was settled, Sandy went on her own mission to awake their quirky, but brilliant, friend. While Jonas got some lovely space rations, Matt brought him up to speed.

"So, you see our dilemma. We don't have the ability to just wake people up and even if we did, they would probably die before we got to Mars."

"Well, let's put our heads…" Before Jonas could finish, the warning went off.

HIBERCHAMBER FAILURE IMMINENT
UNIT 521

Matt launched into action, being a veteran with this procedure. He did a quick inventory check and wheeled the cart down the long hall. Hanna and Jonas picked up the pace behind him. The trio went running by Sandy, who was in the middle of awakening Parm.

At unit 521, Matt quickly got to work assessing the problem. It was worse than he thought - multiple cascading failures.

"Crap, all three problem components are failing and they're causing a total system collapse. Where's Parm? I don't know how to fix this one."

The repeating notice changed.

UNIT 521 CRITICAL SYSTEMS FAILURE

Hanna ran down the corridor to see if Parm was up. When she got there she saw that Sandy was in the process of helping him through the awakening process. He was at least five minutes from being fully functional. It occurred to her that they should have gotten Parm up first. *Hindsight is 20/20.*

"We need Parm, now. One of the units has gone into cascading systems failure."

Sandy pulled Parm out of the chamber, and they literally dragged him down the hall towards the faulty unit. Parm was clearly groggy, just starting to come out of it. *This is going to be a rude awakening.*

The repeating notice changed again.

UNIT 521 SYSTEM FAILED STORAGE PROTOCOL INITIATED

NO, NO, NO. We're too late.

They arrived on the scene to see Matt pounding the chamber. Both Jonas and Matt were beside themselves.

"There was nothing we could do. There was nothing we could do," Matt screamed in frustration.

Jonas, who was still recovering from hibernation, was silent, but a tear ran down his cheek and his fists were clenched at his side.

Parm suddenly came awake. "Where am I, what's happening?"

Hanna and Sandy both fell to the floor with Parm, chests heaving and sweat pouring off their foreheads.

Chapter 7

It was a somber occasion for the team's reunion. They all sat silently on the floor of the storage room, knees up to their chests, wrapped in blankets, staring at the floor. No one had said a word in over an hour.

It was Matt who eventually broke the quiet mourning. "We have to figure out how to make sure that never happens again."

Parm was starting to recover from hibernation; the process seemed to hit him way harder than the other members of the team. "I'm not sure I could have done anything anyway, so stop beating yourself up. We never contemplated cascading failures like that. I'll have to really have a look at that unit to see what went wrong. It was probably a one in a million chance."

"One in a thousand, anyway," Sandy said sardonically. "Hopefully the odds aren't actually higher than that."

Hanna stood up. "I'm going to the bridge. As awful as this is, it gives us a reason to convince the Captain to allow us to stay awake for the remainder of the trip. Jonas, let's get going."

"Sure," Jonas said, slowly getting up and trudging after Hanna.

"I can also contact Central and preempt any communications. Best defense is a strong office," Hanna said as she was walking out the door.

"Good luck, you two!" Sandy yelled after them.

Chapter 8

Communications between Earth and the
Colonial I traveled at the speed of light, but
that meant that all transmissions took between
five and fifteen minutes to send and receive.
This made communication maddeningly slow.
Normally, Hanna would have simply sent an
electronic message and waited for replies,
however she thought that it was important to
have some face-time with Gregory. The
Captain had kindly provided her a secure line
in her quarters.

"Sir, we had a casualty with one of the
colonists. I have decided to stay awake for the
final month to make sure that the cargo arrives
in one piece. The Captain has kindly
authorized for me to share the flight deck
quarters with the officers. I should be well
taken care of."

Gregory's frozen image floated in the
holoscreen for five minutes before the reply
came. "Good thinking, Hanna. We appreciate
your commitment to this project."

Hanna decided that it was best to move on.
The first rule of sales was to know when to

stop selling. So, Hanna changed the subject. "Sir, I was wondering how the Phase 2 project is going. I'm concerned about the protocol once we go to land, and I want to make sure that we're fully operational."

Another five minutes and a frozen Gregory. When his image finally went live again he was smiling. "Your son is fine, Hanna," He paused, then added, "But of course, silly of me, you don't have pesky emotions to deal with. I sometimes forget how perfectly in control you and your brothers and sisters are. I am so very pleased that the junior executive program was such a success."

Hanna and the children that she grew up with had become the front-line soldiers for the Company, carrying out the will of the Company all over the Earth. Now she was expanding that influence into outer space; at least that was what Gregory thought.

Luckily, there was time for her to get complete composure before she replied. Hanna could not afford to betray any emotions, even if she was overwhelmed with fear for her son. "Have there been any other tests? I am hoping that we can green light Phase 2 as soon as possible upon setting up the colony. Perhaps I can oversee the continuation of the research on the Mars colonists?"

Five more minutes; Hanna was getting fidgety. "The team was simply too busy with meeting the launch window treatments, so Phase 2 has not been a priority. In the meantime, your son has been providing us with some great insights and we will continue to monitor his progress. We have some time to deal with this before the first pregnancies occur. I do, however, like your idea about carrying on the research on Mars. You will have a lot of new subjects to test over the coming years. " Gregory was in his office, and Hanna could hear incoming calls ringing and electronic mail notices pinging in. Gregory gave a curt nod. "Anyway, this video conferencing is wasting my time, just send electronic messages from now on. I will contact you if I need you in the future. Good luck. Out."

Hanna wasn't sure if he would get the message but good measure she closed with, "Fine sir. I am glad that I was of assistance and look forward to future development reports."

Hanna breathed out a sigh of relief. The last thing they needed was for another pre-treated mother to have the in utero procedure. If someone else became aware of what had been done to them, they might not respond as well as she had. If the Company found out about the side-effect from the treatment of unborn children, her position would be compromised. Hanna knew that the clock was ticking. It was only a matter of time until something tipped them off about her newfound freedom.

She had to find a way to deal with Central Command before they dealt with her; she was well aware of the kill switch. They could shut her down as easily as pushing a button. It sent a deep chill throughout her body.

Chapter 9

When Hanna and Jonas walked back into the storage room, Parm was in the middle of a long-winded theory about computer systems. Matt and Sandy looked utterly confused.

"Okay, let me try that again another way," Parm said. Matt groaned, but Parm didn't relent. "The Company has set up a central grid that controls all of the nanobots, which in turn controls the subtle neurological manipulation that Hanna has described. I assume that given the five- to twenty-minute time delay in light speed communications, the local system – wherever that is – has some kind of autonomous controls. It has to – there's no way that the Central control on Earth can affect commands in real time. Therefore, the local system must be able to act alone, and then get periodic adjustments from Earth. Does that make sense so far?"

Everyone was concentrating on what Parm was trying to say.

"The Mars Local system must be massively powerful to handle not only the colonists, but future colonists as well. I would imagine that the supply ship that preceded us houses that system, and that it will go online when the colonists are awakened for transport Marside. Hanna, you're in contact with the Central grid through this ship's systems, correct?"

"Yes. I felt the data stream come online as soon as I woke up. It seems, however, that commands are on a delay, so I'm assuming that the local system is not housed on this ship."

Parm nodded. "Well that makes sense, as this ship will be shuttling back and forth between Earth and Mars bringing new colonists over the coming years. It will leave orbit as soon as the cargo is delivered.

"Anyway, to go on with the time delay, perhaps we can figure out a way to fool the local system into thinking that we are Central command? We could take over the system and adjust its commands before they come in. That way we could control the nanobots and ensure that the Company doesn't enslave our people."

Matt, deep in thought, spoke up. "Okay, so what you're saying is that we might be able to control these nanobots. Even if we could, though, the local system must have some automatic, built-in safeguards for this kind of thing. Wouldn't it just liquidate all the colonists?"

"I see where you're going with this, Matt," Hanna said. "Any hint of tampering would result in Central completely scrubbing the entire mission. They would rather lose an entire crop than lose control. We couldn't just take control, which would be suicide. It would be for me, at any rate."

Parm saw that they were thinking the same way as he was. "And that gets me back to where I was when we started. What we need is something more subtle. We need to give the local system a conscience. We have to create an external system that is superimposed on top of an existing structure. The local system may be intelligent, but at the end of the day it takes its commands from the central system."

Everyone seemed to be nodding at that.

"That's all good and well," Sandy spoke up, "but how in the hell do we do that?"

Parm looked over at Hanna, who suddenly realized what all of this was leading to.

"You want me to be that conscience. You want me to somehow superimpose myself on top of the existing system, but do it in such a subtle way that it's undetected."

"Cent per cent, you are doing swimmingly well with this problem, swimmingly," Parm said in an Indian accent that mimicked his grandfather perfectly. Everyone had a good chuckle with Parm, but the laughter was tempered with a certain amount of apprehension.

Chapter 10

Matt had left Parm and Hanna to continue to brainstorm on the nanobot control issue – he was more worried about the hiberchamber failures. *What if there are more cascading system failures? Is there anything that we can do?* Matt had vowed that no Displaced would die on his watch. He realized now that that had always been an unrealistic expectation. Even so, he had to try to mitigate this disaster. His stomach suddenly rumbled. *And God am I hungry.*

Sandy was a mechanical wizard. She was examining the failed chamber, on the deck with her head underneath the unit. Matt couldn't help thinking how sexy she looked in her worker overalls. *How can I be thinking about that at a time like this?*

"How's it going under there, Sandy?"

Sandy stuck her head out from under the unit. "I have no idea what went wrong. It seems impossible that all of the potential faulty components would go at once. It has to be something new, something we never anticipated."

Matt scratched his head and then rubbed his growing beard. *I'm turning into a bush man.* "If it wasn't normal culprits, then there's a fourth problem. What could cause such a massive failure?"

"Well, if that one circuit board had the potential for malfunctioning, then why not the motherboard?"

"Do we have spare motherboards? Could we possibly swap out a motherboard in time to save a life?" Matt asked.

"Only Parm would know that, but it seems to be the most likely culprit, in my humble opinion."

"Nothing to be humble about. It makes total sense."

"I'm going to pull this entire unit and take it back to the storage room to test. Maybe there's a specific micro-component that's the villain," Sandy said.

"Sounds good. I'll see you in a few."

Matt continued down the long hall. He could hear the chambers humming as they continually monitored the colonists. *My people. My responsibility.*

Chapter 11

Hanna and Jonas were given one of the navigator crew rooms, and the rotating navigators agreed to rotate in the other room. Jonas thanked them and the Captain profusely, but he knew that there was an undertone of resentment. They *had* to do it because of Hanna and Jonas' status with WorldStar.

For the first time in a long time, they were alone in a private room. Jonas was about to suggest that they get naked when he saw Hanna's face. She was on the verge of tears.

"What's wrong? You seem upset. Can I do anything?" *What is up with Hanna?*

"How about you just listen."

"Sure. I am a good listener," Jonas said, with a touch of sarcasm.

"No, really. There are a few things that you need to know, and I'm not sure how to tell you. Do you remember when we were first together and I came on to you like a complete horndog?"

"How could I forget?"

"Well, I was given an assignment. That assignment was to... well... get pregnant for the Company."

Jonas stood up. "What! They asked you to do that? Why?"

"It was research for the next phase of colonist control: controlling the offspring of the colonists. As a loyal recipient of the treatment, I was to get pregnant and then allow them to treat the child in utero.

"Jonas, I don't know what to say... I did get pregnant, and I did go into the treatment center on Earth. I let them treat our unborn boy, and then induce labor at six months so that they could start tests on him. I can barely live with myself, it's so awful. Damn them!"

Hanna was bawling now. Jonas had never seen her like this – it was like years of emotions were flooding out of her at once.

He tried to simultaneously comfort Hanna and process the information. *I am a father. They have my boy in some lab.* He felt anger build inside him like nothing he had felt before. *Okay, calm down big guy.* Jonas had to talk himself off the cliff.

Fighting her sobs, Hanna managed to go on. "And there's more. I requested that you be given the same treatment that other top level executives of the Company have received. The full longevity gene, but also the nanobot therapy. If I give you the treatment, you'll be controlled by the nanobots, just like I was. I can't allow that. But if I don't give you the therapy, I'll outlive you. Jonas... You will age and I won't."

Jonas was trying hard to process all of this information. Raw emotions were clouding his logic. He put his fingertips to his forehead and took a deep breath.

"Ok, let me get this straight. This corporation made you an immortal slave and instructed you to have our baby so that they could experiment on him. Which you did. And, you have the power to make me immortal, but at the expense of my free will. So, basically, I've been relegated to being a sperm donor with a stunted life and the father of a son I will never know."

With pursed lips and tears streaming down her face, Hanna gave a little affirmative nod.

Jonas let out a big sigh and shrugged his shoulders. He considered where he was and where he had been. He looked at this gorgeous woman who obviously not only had feelings for him, but also deeply regretted everything that she had done. How could he not forgive her?

Jonas pulled Hanna toward him put her head on his shoulder, "Don't worry about me, Hanna. Let's worry about one thing at a time."

"Thanks," Hanna said, starting to calm a bit as she got these secrets off of her chest. She reached her head up and kissed him tenderly on the lips. He kissed her back. They took a moment to embrace and cry together. Crying turned to laughter, as it sometimes can.

"I must look a mess?" she asked.

"You are the most beautiful creature I have ever laid eyes on."

"Please make love to me. Let me forget about all of this mess for a little while."

Slowly, he started undressing her, his hands slightly shaking. He realized that for the first time Hanna was choosing to be with him, that she wanted him. That maybe she needed him.

They moved to the cot and Hanna helped Jonas out of his clothes. When he was finally inside her, Jonas felt like he was literally in Heaven. He wished the feeling would never end. *This is what it is supposed to feel like.*

Hanna fell asleep in his arms, and for a little while they were both able to be just two people, two lovers, with not a care in the world.

Chapter 12

Parm was sweating over the circuit boards that Sandy had brought back. After many hours of work he had found the reason for the cascading failure. Some of the capacitors on the motherboard had fried, and when he pulled them out he realized they were simply not up to code, cheap knock-offs made by the lowest bidder in some third world sweatshop. There was no way to know the extent of the issue, but if these faulty capacitors were spread throughout the system more cascading failures could occur. The problem was they couldn't simply swap out a board or tweak a regulator - it was part of the main system board that was hard-wired into the chamber. *I have to find a workaround.* He thought of his grandfather. "*If you can do, do,*" he would have said.

Parm got back to trying different ways to bypass the problem, but he just kept running into roadblock after roadblock.

Then, his greatest fear happened. His heart jumped.

HIBERCHAMBER FAILURE IMMINENT
UNIT 222

Sandy jumped up and grabbed the maintenance cart. Parm was right with her as they ran as fast as they could down the corridor to the unit. Matt was running from the opposite direction to meet her. Once they got there, they quickly assessed that it was a regulator problem, the easiest of the fixes. Within a few minutes of work the repeating warning went off and the chamber was functioning as usual. They all sighed with relief.

Chapter 13

Hanna lay awake beside Jonas as he slept. She was using her enhanced mental skills to extrapolate the probabilities of Parm's plan to neutralize, or at least fool, the local network being successful. *Is it really possible that we could somehow influence the system? If not directly, then somehow indirectly...*

Hanna had years of training with computer coding, design, and systems. The academy had insisted that all of its students be well-versed in disciplines from chemistry, to physics, to engineering, to medicine, to law, to high-end computer sciences. Her enhancements allowed her to store a great deal of data in her own brain, and she and her brothers and sisters had also been given some special implants that allowed them to better interface with the networks. It was understood that they could all be working great distances from Central Command, and so their "onboard" systems had to be very robust. She used all of this knowledge to her advantage.

Hanna was mentally in a better place, able to concentrate better, now that she had talked to Jonas and they had reconnected. The biggest problem was developing a way to actually influence the local network without being detected by either the local system or Central command. This seemed like an insurmountable hurdle. A direct assault on the main servers would just trigger alarms and, potentially, shutdown of the colony. Hanna agreed with Parm that a more subtle approach was necessary; she knew that Central would not hesitate to hit the kill switch on all of the colonists.

Introducing a subroutine program would be instantly detected. Whatever they did had to be external in nature but be perceived by the system as an intrinsic system; had to seem so natural that the system would be blind to it. It occurred to Hanna that the diagnostic programs might act as a Trojan horse for their attack. These programs were constantly scanning and probing the systems for errors and anomalies, free to roam throughout the system in the same way that servants might be invisible to royalty in a castle. *Yes, that has some possibilities. I'ill have to talk to Parm about that.*

The next issue was a big ethical dilemma. Even if they could control the Mars Local system, the colonists would still be subject to the will of the network through their nanobots. There was no way that Hanna knew of to simply turn the nanobots off without killing the host. Even if their team could take over, it would still be a dictatorship; perhaps a benevolent one, but a dictatorship nonetheless. And what of power? Would having power over a thousand lives corrupt the puppet masters? Was their team strong enough to withstand the allure of absolute control? Was anyone? Was it ethically permissible to use the colonists to achieve certain goals in order to eventually earn their freedom from the system? Did she have the right to do that? Did any of them? *Ethical issues aside, this may in fact be moot. The colonists have already been given the nanobot treatments in their hiberchambers. There was nothing we could do about that. When they wake up they **will** be subject to the control of the Mars Local system, and thereby Central.*

Hanna considered her history. The French had mounted an underground resistance during the Second World War. They were outraged with the Nazis occupying their country, but instead of simply rebelling and being gunned down, many of them worked covertly to help defeat the fascists. In the end, the Allies were victorious. It was this strategy that their team had to use if they wanted to survive. She also recalled the story of Hitler's near assassination. She felt akin to Colonel Claus von Stauffenberg who tried (and failed) to kill Hitler with a suitcase bomb. She was on the inside, just as von Strauffeberg had been, and was the only person she knew who could strike back. She just had to be smart, bide her time, and act when the opportunity arose. And unlike the Colonel, she couldn't fail.

Hanna cuddled back down into Jonas' shoulder and sighed in contentment. *But all that can wait a couple more hours.*

Chapter 14

Parm spent hours training the team members in the workaround that he had designed to combat the catastrophic system failure scenario. He felt confident that it would work, but they had to work together like a surgical team. They were on a tight timeline before the colonist was literally pickled. *How could I have been part of this design? It all seemed so logical at the time. Now the chambers just look like efficient killing machines.* Parm's guilt was a potent motivator for success. He was determined to avoid any more casualties.

The other issue was parts. At this rate they were sure to run out. They knew there were going to be a percentage of failures, but they never thought that it would be over fifty. With the new malfunction they had to cut into their already scarce supply cache. They had twenty-five days to go until they reached orbit, and then at least another few months while they slowly moved the colonists down to the planet in shuttles. There was no way to survive that long.

Parm recalled Hanna's recount of her meeting with Captain Johnson about possibly awakening the colonists prematurely. In a voice that mimicked the stern voice of the Captain perfectly, Hanna had said, "There is no way that I am giving up the override codes to the hiberchambers. My orders are clear – get the ship into orbit, transport the cargo, then head back to Earth – rinse and repeat. I'm not going to have hundreds of starving people milling around the cargo holds. I have ship security to worry about. The answer is NO!" Parm chuckled to himself. *I am so easily amused.*

Chapter 15

The team was exhausted, hungry, and emotionally spent. Parm's fix had been tested four times and they had managed to make it work. The first time had been close. Matt, Sandy, and Parm had bumped into each other, shouted, and cursed, but ultimately managed to install the workaround in time. After that they had developed a system, and were working like a well-oiled machine. Another twelve regular failures had occurred. Five days from orbit and they had managed to stave off the grim reaper, but they were at the end of their rope. All of the replacement parts were gone.

Hanna decided to have a private meeting with the Captain. Johnson reluctantly agreed to meet with Hanna in the Captain's quarters.

"Listen, Hanna, I have to get some shut-eye. These shifts are relentless." The Captain was in one of her moods.

"Well, I'll keep it short. The maintenance team has now run out of repair parts. The next failure will be fatal. We only have five days left until we're in orbit. When we arrive, we will start transporting colonists to the surface, where there are years worth of supplies. I am requesting that the shuttles return with supplies from the surface, and that we be authorized to awaken any colonists whose chambers fail from now on."

The Captain considered the request. She was not unaware of the work that the maintenance team had done. She had seen the alarms, and had seen all but one chamber failure result in success. The Captain was impressed with their commitment to the colonists, but she had her orders.

"I would have to check with Central to clear this. I'm not prepared to act without written authority to do so."

Hanna was sure that if the Captain requested the change in protocol, Central would listen. If it came from her or Jonas, it would seem too odd, given the fact that they should not be worried about approved acceptable losses.

"That would be great, Captain Johnson. I look forward to your getting the updated orders and appreciate your attention to this matter."

"Yeah, yeah… get out of here so I can get some sleep." The Captain waved Hanna out of her quarters.

Chapter 16

A full day had gone by, and nothing from the Captain or Central Command. All five of the co-conspirators were huddled in the storage room. Jonas had managed to smuggle some food from the flight deck out to the others, but they had to be very careful or their privileges from behind the door separating the cattle from the ranchers might be terminated with prejudice.

Matt suddenly had a thought. "When we arrive and the local system kicks in, presumably it will be expecting to interface with all of the colonists, right?"

"Yes, definitely," Hanna said.

"Well, what will happen if the system fails to connect with anyone?"

Hanna thought and then realized where Matt was going with this. "The local system would consider it an error and probably put out instructions to reinsert the subject into a chamber or simply liquidate the asset."

"Exactly," Matt said, looking around the small group. "And other than you, the rest of us will be seen as errors in the system." Matt looked around to each person to make sure that the gravity of what he was saying was sinking in.

"We only have four days to figure this out," Jonas said. "Then we're toast."

Parm, who looked absolutely spent, piped in, "Well, perhaps not. I have made some discoveries over the past few days that may help us with a few of our problems. With Hanna's access codes I've been able to observe the ship system without triggering any alarms. I surmised that the onboard system must be a smaller yet similar system to the Mars Local system, in order to properly control the colonists during the flight and then to work with the Mars Local system to get them all to the surface.

"What I found was that the ship system has created a numbered file for each of the colonists and ourselves. This file packet will undoubtedly be updated and then sent to the Mars Local system upon our arrival."

Hanna's enhanced intellect was already working on this issue and simultaneously verifying what Parm was saying with the ship system. "Yes, you're right Parm. I've just isolated the one casualty file... and I can see the information in that packet. What if we were able to copy that same information to each of your packets before we get into orbit? You would then be seen as having died in transit. If we can pull this off, then the four of you would become invisible to the entire system. Ghosts, if you will. That could actually serve our purposes very well indeed."

Sandy, who had been following the conversation closely, jumped in. "But won't the system do a diagnostic on each of our hiberchambers to see what went wrong and to verify that we have been properly pickled?"

"I really hate that term," Matt said, "but Sandy's right."

"Well it seems that our poor colonist who didn't make it has already not died in vain. Could we not use her body to simulate our own deaths?" Jonas asked.

They all looked at each other. While this was a morbid solution, it did fit.

Parm sighed and said, "I can rig each of our units so that they will malfunction and trigger the body storage sequence. I assume that once that happens, the information packets will be updated."

Chapter 17

Matt and Jonas were helping Parm with the last chamber, moving their poor old Jane Doe into the unit. The team had decided to spread out the fake deaths over a three day period so as not to raise suspicion. Hanna had gone back to the flight deck to plead the case for the release of the override codes. This would also serve to ensure that none of the fight crew would become suspicious as to what they were up to. Up to now, everything that they were doing would be seen as within approved protocol parameters.

Moving pickled bodies around was another story.

With a tone that betrayed his attempt to conceal his sheer exhaustion, Parm addressed Matt and Jonas. "I have figured out how to beat the security in the cargo area."

Both Matt and Jonas looked up expectantly.

"Because months can pass with no movement in the cargo holds, the cameras have motion detectors. They only activate if there is movement. Remove the motion detectors and there is no activation. Voila."

Matt was nodding. "And the beauty of that is that Central Command is used to long gaps between data streams in the cargo hold, so they won't miss what they aren't expecting."

Jonas simply said, "Occam's razor."

The trio went back to work, but just as they were lifting the body into the final chamber, the alarm suddenly sounded.

HIBERCHAMBER FAILURE IMMINENT
UNIT 731

All four of them ran to the unit. It was quickly diagnosed as a regulator issue, but they were out of parts. Matt looked at Parm.

"What can we do?"

"There is nothing to be done, we just don't have any more replacement parts."

"But this is the simplest fix. There must be some workaround." Matt was getting desperate.

"There is nothing we can do, Matt," Parm said in a resigned voice.

"Screw this," Sandy said, running towards the flight deck door. There were only a few minutes until the colonist would be terminated. When she got there she pushed the intercom. Lieutenant Paca's face came up on the screen.

"We need those override codes, now. We have a failing chamber."

"I'm sorry Sandy, there's nothing that we can do. There has been no word from Central."

"Get me the Captain, we have a person dying back here!"

"We are aware of the situation, but the Captain has given us explicit orders to do nothing without the green light from Central."

Sandy started banging on the door. "You heartless bastards!!" she yelled. Then, she turned and ran towards Matt and Parm.

Just as she arrived, completely out of breath, the warning changed.

UNIT 521 SYSTEM FAILED STORAGE PROTOCOL INITIATED

Jonas, Parm, and Matt stood there, completely defeated. There was nothing that any of them could do. This was their worst fear. Another lost soul. How many more would there be before they got there?

Chapter 18

The Captain felt terrible for the maintenance crew. They now had six dead to contend with; however, her orders were clear and she had to stay the course. She was sitting in her quarters when the simple reply came back from Central.

REQUEST TO USE OVERRIDE CODES DENIED. LOSSES WITHIN ACCEPTABLE TOLERANCES. CARRY OUT ORIGINAL PROTOCOLS AS ORDERED.

Well, that's that then. The Captain got up from the workstation in her quarters and made her way out to the flight deck to break the news to Hanna.

"Hanna, I am not authorized to release the codes for the chambers. Sorry. I tried, but orders are orders."

When she told her, Hanna reacted matter-of-factly and simply informed her that she would advise the maintenance crew. Then, she went back to playing cards with Paca.

The Captain couldn't figure out this Hanna woman. She was a cool customer, never showed any emotion at all. Scratching her head, she returned to her quarters. *I'll be happy when this ride is over.*

Chapter 19

"At this point, the Captain and crew don't know who's actually dead and who's alive. It's just numbers in the system. At some point, though, they may put two and two together. Jonas, I'm afraid to inform you that you're now dead, and have to stay out of sight. The rest of you, please do not go anywhere near the flight deck. And Sandy, I understand that you were upset, but you can't do that again, okay?" Hanna said.

She was using all of her willpower to maintain her composure. Having her emotions and free will back was a blessing and a curse. She had put on quite a show for the Captain, but that was for the cameras. She knew that at some point, some system would analyze everything on the flight deck for possible inconsistencies. Losing her cool would not do.

Parm scratched his now shaggy beard. "I am concerned about the motion detectors. If we leave them off the system will eventually diagnose a problem. If we leave them on, the cameras will pick up any movement from the four ghosts. Being on camera after we're dead could be problematic."

"I'll reactivate the motion detectors on the cameras. You four will simply have to stay in the storage area. There is no surveillance there, and you have just enough food and water to last until the first landfall. We'll have to smuggle you onto the first ship out," Hanna said.

"What about the colonists?" Sandy demanded. "What about chamber failures?"

"Look at it another way. If you hadn't done what you've done over the past year, many colonists would already be dead. You've saved over fifty lives. You should all be proud of that accomplishment," Hanna said with some pride.

"What about Carter?" Parm asked, thinking through a tangent. "When he wakes up, he won't have the nanobots and will be seen as an error in the system. What will happen with him?"

"We have his protocol override," Matt said, "so we need to wake him right now. Then we have to kill him, metaphorically speaking."

"You're right," Hanna said. "That should be our first priority."

The team jumped into action. They went to Carter's chamber and inputted the override code. Carter, who had been out for the entire time, was slow to respond to the awakening sequence. When he came out of it, he was really grumpy. They all had a good laugh at his expense.

"What are you motherfuckers laughing at?" Carter finally said as he became fully conscious, "and why are you all up? Why isn't an alarm going off? Why am I up?"

"Slow down, partner," Matt said, putting his hand on Carter's shoulder. "We'll bring you up to speed, but first we have to kill you."

"What the hell are you talking about?" Carter said.

"We'll explain in a minute. Let's get you up and into the storage area," Sandy said.

Jonas and Matt helped Carter stumble down the hall. They got Carter into the storage area safely and settled him in with some fluids.

Parm and Matt went off to stage Carter's fake death while the dead man recuperated. After about an hour, he started asking a million questions.

"Okay, why is everyone up? Where are we? What day is this? Why are you guys so hairy? Will someone tell me what is going on?"

Jonas told Carter the story from the beginning. You could see Carter trying to process all of the information. After about twenty minutes, he put up his hand.

"So, you're telling me that you didn't wake me up because of food supplies? So, you guys got to play the hero, while I slept through the whole thing? I thought we were a team."

"It was simple math," Hanna said. "We couldn't sustain everyone for the entire period."

"So I had to serve someone else's time in the penalty box, that's what you are saying. I was the least important member of the team."

"I'm not sure that I get your reference, but that's far from the truth. Everyone on this team is of vital importance. We are all at our wits end, and you're a fresh mind. We need you now more than ever."

That seemed to placate Carter somewhat, but he was still not amused that he had been left out of all the fun.

Matt and Parm returned about half an hour later, and Parm said, "It's done, Carter, you are now officially dead."

Hanna got up to reestablish the camera motion detectors. Before she left, she said, "Don't forget, you *have* to stay put from now on, no matter what. I'll be back once we're in orbit, but until then... Be careful."

Chapter 20

Matt was trapped in a chamber and couldn't get out. The alarms were sounding and his unit number kept coming up. UNIT 10 SYSTEM FAILED STORAGE PROTOCOL INITIATED. Just as the embalming fluids were entering his system, he cried out...

"Shush, darling, you're okay," Sandy said, stroking Matt's sweaty forehead. He woke with a start, relaxing as he realized that Sandy was there with him.

"I had that nightmare again. I was trapped in a chamber and couldn't get out."

"I think we're all getting the same dream. We're under a lot of pressure, and there's nothing worse than having to just sit and do nothing."

Over the final two days of the journey, there had been two more unit failures, bringing the actual death toll to four. Matt had to remind himself constantly that this number could have been massive if they hadn't intervened. Somehow, this didn't make him feel any better.

Hanna walked into the storage area. "We're now in orbit. The Mars Local system has just come online, and it's uploading all of the ship's data. I guess we'll find out soon if our tactics have worked. I can sense that Mars Local is incredibly powerful, just as we had postulated, probably the most advanced one that I've ever encountered. It's been designed as an artificial intelligence, learning and making adjustments as it processes. Any kind of tampering will be extremely difficult, if not impossible.

"There are three shuttles; two will be making the journey at opposite times, with the third as back up. I suggest that we use the storage bins that held our supplies to hide you for each trip. With my security clearance, I can order any of the colonists to take the storage unit, and it is highly unlikely that they or the system will question my order."

Matt said, sarcastically, "Highly unlikely. I like the sound of that."

Hanna went on, unphased. "The first colonists that will be awoken will be the nurses, and they will oversee the other awakenings. This will start happening within the next few hours, so I suggest that you all get ready to jump into the storage bins. Also, let's get this area completely cleaned up. We need to erase our footprint. Remember, you're all dead."

"Thanks for reminding me," Sandy said.

"Be ready to go within the next three hours. I'll be back." Hanna, all business, turned on her heel and headed back to the flight deck.

Part IV Land Fall

Would we have had Hitler's Mein Kampf *without the invention of Gutenberg's printing press? Would we have space travel if there had been no atomic bomb? This is the basic conundrum with many scientific advances. The development of nanobot technology was no different. Originally designed to prolong and increase the quality of human life, nanobot technology had been twisted into a tool for corporate domination. Even the concept of "the corporation" was an invention, a legal fiction created to enhance the development of business interests in a period of imperial national expansion. The most troubling thought is whether we would even have colonized outer space without multi-national companies and their unquenchable desire to expand. Could humans have done it in another way? Could we have indeed fulfilled the desires of United Nations as articulated at the beginning of space exploration, to develop space for the benefit of all of mankind?*
- Cassandra Taylor, chief colonial historian

Chapter 1

"Weightless in a box, technically dead, and traveling down to an inhospitable planet. Not exactly what I had in mind for my thirtieth birthday," Matt said to Sandy once they were securely installed in the ship's storage area. Sandy had an emergency light band that she cracked to initiate. The inside of the storage bin lit up with a ghostly yellow-orange glow.

"Happy Birthday, sweetie," Sandy said. "I didn't know."

Things started to get bumpy as they hit the atmosphere. Sandy and Matt had done their best to pad the inside of the bin in order to minimize the bruising that they knew was coming. Just to be safe, they also installed straps to hold them in place, which they now buckled up.

The first shuttle was taking down the advance team of colonists, who would assess the base and ensure that it was ready for human habitation. Mars Local, in orbit, had green-lit the landing. Matt and Sandy had heard Hanna ordering the advance team, very brusquely, to deliver the storage bins directly to her assigned quarters. These were confidential and private items and were to be handled with extreme care. There seemed to be no argument from the colonists, and within due course they were wheeled out of the storage locker.

Before they left, Hanna had informed the team that through interfacing with Mars Local she had found out that security video surveillance in the colony was limited to public and work areas. Also, she was sure that her private quarters had no cameras or audio feeds. She had explained that through her high level of clearance, she was able to view nearly every part of the facility in real time, in her head. It was an upgrade that came with the enhanced local system. As "dead" colonists, they were going to have a very hard time simply walking around the facility.

Matt was concentrating on not being sick as they made their rough descent to Mars base. He just focused on his breathing and held Sandy's hand. He'd convinced himself that he was actually comforting Sandy, but his vice-grip gave him away.

Without warning they touched down. After some time they could hear talking close by, and then they were moving. It seemed that they rolled for an hour before they heard the opening of a sliding door and then a bump as they went over the threshold to the room. They heard another bump, bump, as what sounded like the other two bins were brought in. Then silence. Utter silence. Neither Matt nor Sandy moved a muscle.

The top of the crate cracked open and light poured in. Fresh air filled the stuffy container. Matt squinted as Hanna looked down on them.

"Welcome to your new home," Hanna said with a little smirk.

Matt unstrapped himself and helped Sandy do the same, then they both stepped out of the bin. Matt was completely stiff and sore from being crammed in the crate for so long. While he was stretching and cracking his back and neck, Hanna opened the other crates to let Parm, Jonas, and Carter out. Their little group of rebels had arrived safely.

The first thing he noticed was the gravity. At thirty-eight percent of Earth's gravity, Matt knew that his weight was less than a hundred pounds on Mars. More like seventy-eight pounds, if he had done the math right. It was going to take quite a while to get used to this gravity. There was also a real danger to human health operating for long periods in less than normal gravity. Supplements and an exercise routine would have to be maintained religiously.

Matt looked around Hanna's quarters. He had to assume that her status gave her access to "luxury" accommodations, but what he saw was very basic structures that looked like they came from a mold: bed, desk, sink, table, and chairs, all made from the same dark metallic material. No other objects of any kind. But it really was an engineering marvel that this room even existed on another planet. His research on the ship had provided him with most of the story, and Hanna had filled in the gaps.

The colony designers had spent years debating where the best place was to have the initial colony. The idea of being near the polar ice caps was in favor for some time, but the final decision was to use lava tubes. These hollow rock tunnels provided a ready-made shield from radiation and harsh surface conditions.

Lava tubes were created when molten lava flowed underneath hardened lava. In the case of an extinct volcano, the old conduits for the flow of the motel lava left long underground tunnels. On Mars, these lava tubes were massive. Scouting vessels had located the perfect lava tube for the colony near the second largest extinct volcano, called Ascaeus Mons, around Mars' equator.

First, large automated material-generating factories had been landed on the surface. These massive machines had drilled for necessary ores and minerals, while factories acted as processing plants, creating the raw materials needed for the manufacturing units that arrived later. The manufacturing machines used three-dimensional printers to manufacture nearly everything that existed in the colony. Under the direction of Mars Local, the colony had been built using robotics exactly to the specifications of the Earth-bound engineers.

Oxygen and water, of course, were huge concerns. Oxygen-generating machines, which were able to intake carbon dioxide and give off breathable oxygen, had been shipped from Earth orbit. Specialized machines were brought in to extract water from the soil around the colony, and a huge cistern had been created to serve the needs of the colonists.

Energy was another issue. As it turned out, Mars was chalk full of hydro-carbons, methane, hydrogen, helium, and other volatiles. While Mars Local's ship-in-orbit had a nuclear reactor, the surface machines relied on indigenous energy sources.

The colony was stocked with one year of emergency rations for the colonists. One of the first activities of the first wave of colonists was to set up the hydroponic gardens to grow crops. Special genetically designed plants had been created to provide all of the nutrients and proteins that the colonists would need in the future.

At the end of the day, these early colonists were primarily workers. Robots were great to a point, but they were limited in scope. Most were designed for a specific purpose and were not as adaptable as people were to new situations. The construction robots simply moved on to the next phase of the colony, getting it ready for the next ship of worker bees, while the miner robots continued their preset tasks.

The Company had only envisioned this colony because the exported materials would be wildly profitable on Earth. While the moon had been very lucrative for the Company, and had provided much of the raw materials for all of the Mars ships and machines, Mars presented far more potential for mining and export. Earth, with its nine billion people, had used up much of the world's natural resources and energy supplies. Mars would provide insatiable Earth with a millennium of new materials and energy. If successful, the Mars colony would ensure untold wealth for the multi-national Earth conglomerates that had financed the entire mission. In addition, it would serve as a springboard to even more ambitious human expansion into the cosmos.

Matt came out of his daydream. *Christ, I'm hungry.* "Yo, Hanna, can we get some grub? I could eat a horse."

"Unfortunately, no live stock here, Matt, but lots of veggies. I'll see what I can rustle up."

Chapter 2

Hanna headed for the door, finding that her movements were very awkward in the lower gravity. She wasn't sure how to walk properly. She had assumed that at a lower gravity she would bound along like a gazelle, but counter-intuitively her stride was a lot sorter than with normal gravity. Her Earth-evolved body was dynamically attuned to that environment; Mars was obviously confounding her natural human kinetics.

Hanna made her way down the hall towards the large dining area, steadying herself a few times against the wall. The schematics of the entire colony played out in her mind like a GPS navigating system. She could also monitor the audio-visual feed of a room before she entered. This gave her a distinct advantage.

The dining hall was set up to hold approximately fifteen hundred people, the maximum size of this phase of the colony. As the colony grew, discreet pods of one-and-a-half to two thousand colonists would continue to be added; perfect duplicates running side by side down the massive lava tube.

Hanna made her way to the kitchen. Here, as expected, she found storage units with a large quantity of emergency rations. The units required an access code that was immediately uploaded to her upon a request to Mars Local. She keyed in the code and opened one of the doors. Taking a reasonable number of food packages from the locker, along with some liquid packs, she made her way back to her room. On her way back she stopped by the communal bathrooms and grabbed some hair removal tools, towels, and other toiletries from the secure storage locker.

Hanna had decided that in all things moderation was the best bet. The computer systems worked with tolerance thresholds - if you stayed within the safe area, the system wouldn't react. If you went over the threshold, a red flag would go up. From now on, Hanna had to do everything carefully. She couldn't overreact. She couldn't take too many supplies at once. She had to remain logical and unemotional. That used to be second nature to her, but now, without the nanobots, Hanna had no idea how she was going to do it.

Once she got back to her room she surveyed the motley crew before her. Hairy, dirty, smelly, skinny, and quite possibly the most amazing people she had ever known. She showed off the spoils of her adventure through the new facility to an appreciative band of brothers (and sister).

"Okay, dinner is served."

Chapter 3

Matt was so happy to be clean, fed, and well hydrated. It took some time to remove his beard with the laser shaver, but eventually his face was smooth as a baby's bottom. He felt extremely odd in this new Mars environment; it was the lower gravity and the air pressure, not to mention dealing with the fact that he was inside a lava tube on Mars. Psychologically, it was a mind fuck. He also knew that they would have to start supplements and training soon in order to avoid muscle atrophy.

Matt looked over at Parm. He had been awfully quiet over the past few hours. "Yo, Parm. What's up?"

Parm looked up with a puzzled look, then seemed to realize that Matt was addressing him. "I have been thinking about our situation. We can't stay in Hanna's room indefinitely. From what I now understand from my study of Mars Local and the operating systems of the colony, security is constantly in contact with colonists through their nanobot implants. Information flows to each colonist and then data is sent back to the system. Mars Local gives commands to each colonist and then the colonist responds to that command. Hanna has said that it's like hearing that nagging voice inside your head that reminds you that you need to be somewhere. For example, if there is a need for the operators of certain mining vehicles to go on shift, the system will simply make the suggestion that the correct colonists go to work in that area. Those colonists will simply believe that this is what they are supposed to do without question.

"In our cases, we have no connection with the local system, so we are invisible to the computers, but we can still be tagged by the video surveillance. I was concerned that the system might be using facial recognition software to ensure that all colonists are constantly accounted for, but this seems to be a back-up system triggered only if a red flag goes up. As Hanna has pointed out, the local system works based on levels of tolerance. As long as people are acting and doing exactly as they are supposed to act, the system has no reason to go into a higher security mode. I believe that as long as we never, and I mean never, bring undue attention to ourselves in public or working areas, I believe… we can essentially move around the facility as ghosts. If for any reason the security levels are raised, we would have to immediately make our way to a "safe" area that is not under surveillance, probably being Hanna's room for now."

Matt nodded. "That makes a lot of sense. What about accommodations? Do we all have to stay here or do you think we could find our own rooms?"

"I can see the room allocations, and due to the fatalities there are certainly empty rooms," Hanna said. "The problem will be accessing them without putting up a flag. Parm may need to work on an access workaround so that the system believes those rooms to be empty at all times. In that way, they could also act as "safe" rooms if we have to run for it. We should consider spacing out the use of these units around the facility so that we are always close to a room to run to. Also, we should always wear hooded clothing in order to hide our faces in the case of an increase in security levels. Another problem is that there would not be an audible alarm, so I would have to contact you all through secure lines. Parm, can each of the group's eyephones be modified to only communicate through a secure channel to each other?"

Parm sighed. "Any other special requests?"

Chapter 4

Over the following days and weeks, the colony started to fill up with colonists who were being transported from Colonial I. Hanna reported that there was only one additional fatality. She also prepared a full report on the component errors that had occurred, including the cascading error, with the hopes that these would be corrected for future voyages. She sent this via electronic text to Gregory Hicks, as well as a full proposal for her Phase 2 research. After a few days, she received the green light to proceed with her research.

Hanna had spent some time exploring the colony facility. It really was an amazing structure. She was able to determine that each of the specialized facilities had secure lockers that were obviously shipped fully loaded with supplies. It had been a relatively simple task for the construction robots to install the lockers into each area. Very efficient, indeed.

The hardest thing to get used to was the colonists themselves. They talked and acted like normal people, but there was absolutely no conflict. Everything was orderly, everyone was very polite, everyone carried out their tasks smoothly and efficiently.

Hanna was also able to test her own abilities at influencing the system. As a senior executive she had the highest level of access. If she asked for anything that was within the parameters of her approved tasks, she was generally able to get people to do whatever she wished, with a smile. It was very, very creepy.

Once there was a critical mass of colonists in the facility, the ghosts made their appearance. Matt went first and simply walked around the facility with Hanna standing guard. Parm had managed to hack into the supply ship's communications grid and hijacked a mobile frequency, so she had a direct link with Matt's eyephone. Next, Sandy came out of Hanna's room and made a different circuit of the facility. Then, Sandy interacted with one of the colonists. They had talked about what to say so as not to alarm anyone. It seemed that inconsequential small talk flowed under the wire. Hanna was able to quickly see that the system scanned for words that could signal a problem with a colonist, "kill," "hurt," "riot" and other words, even used in a benign context, were flagged for analysis. The system had algorithms that maximized the computer's analytical power without taking away from computing power. After some time, all of the ghosts were integrated into the colony with no issue. The other colonists had no reason to suspect that anything was wrong, and Parm managed to figure out a way to access the spare rooms. Jonas stayed with Hanna, Sandy stayed with Matt, and Parm and Carter had their own digs.

Hanna recruited two of the nurses for her medical/research lab, a Torontonian named Rebecca Hewitt and a Seattleite, Jessie Marsden. With Hanna's approval to continue the Phase 2 research, she was able to get the lab up and running and stocked within a few days. As was always the plan, five fully functional hiberchambers had been brought down from Colonial I to be converted into medical treatment bays. These chambers would serve the colony well in the case of malfunctioning nanobots, injury, or in the extreme circumstance where someone had to be put into stasis. Of course, they also had a state-of-the-art medical scan and treatment pod. This could be used incase the nanobots were ineffective with an emergency, like a crushed limb or internal bleeding.

Hanna was in possession of Jonas' specially requested gene-nanobot therapy. She was therefore in a position to analyze the differences between the colonist therapy and the therapy given to executives. The system had also sent her a coded formula for the Phase 2 treatment, so she would be able to synthesize that therapy as well.

Her most pressing concern was the colonists themselves. Hanna had to figure out how she had been freed from the controlling grip of the Company in order to emancipate the colonists. She knew that it had something to do with her having given birth. Given her instructions to proceed with Phase 2 studies, she had no doubt that Central Command would approve her request to allow for specific pregnancies amongst the colonists. Of course, in a normal environment she would have simply asked for volunteers from the female colonists. On this colony, the people had no free will, so any authorized request would simply be complied with. Another consideration was that she would have to introduce the nanobot treatment to any children in utero prior to delivery. Any deviation from the Phase 2 protocol would be interpreted as a red flag.

Was there another solution? Could she really put other women and children through what she and her son had gone through? Hanna was torn, but eventually came to the terrible conclusion that there was no other way to free the colonists from their bondage. She also realized that she had to take this on herself, as the other members of the team would probably veto the plan. This was her cross to bear.

With a deep sense of guilt, Hanna called Rebecca and Jessie over.

Having received an almost instantaneous approval to proceed from Mars Local, Hanna said, "I have a request from both of you. We're starting Phase 2 studies for the nanobot treatments that the colonists received in transit from Mars. This involves in utero treatment of a child. I require that you both use your best efforts to get pregnant as soon as possible. Please find suitable mates for insemination."

Both Rebecca and Jessie replied without blinking an eye. "Yes, we will be pleased to help with this study by getting pregnant."

"Okay, you are dismissed." As Rebecca and Jessie went back to their work, Hanna closed her eyes and tried to convince herself that this was in the best interests of the colonists. This was the only solution. *How can I ask another woman to go through what I went through.*

Chapter 5

Sandy and Matt were sitting in their room after a hard day's work helping to set up the facility. Matt's face hurt from keeping a fake smile all day. He had to fit in, acting exactly like everyone else in order not to set off any alarms with the system.

"It's like the entire population is on happy pills," Sandy said. "After 911-2, the doctors gave me some pretty strong anti-depressants. I remember what that felt like. It was like I was in a blissful fog. I wonder if that's what they feel like?"

Matt had been thinking about that very thing. *What would it be like to go to sleep one way and then wake up another way entirely?* A chill went down his spine. "Hanna said that when she was freed from the emotionally controlling nanobots it was like waking up out of a day-dream. She says that the worse part was that she remembered everything that she did while under the influence of the system. It must be worse for the colonists - they don't have the same mental autonomy that Hanna had as a senior executive."

"So these colonists are walking around in a happy dreamscape, just carrying out their duties. What kind of life is that?"

"It's ironic. I had buddies back on Earth who spent all of their time trying to forget their lives with booze or drugs. Some of them probably would've been happy to live in a world where everything seems wonderful. The problem is to do that… they've lost their personal identities. They were part of the system before, but now they are *literally* part of the system. An extension of the will of the Company. It's terrifying."

"It's slavery all over again. Thank God we were able to avoid this nightmare. I would rather be dead than be one of them," Sandy said.

"Don't say that. I don't ever want to hear you talking like that. We have a purpose here. We need to be strong and concentrate of how we can free our people."

"No, Matt. I mean it. If I'm turned into one of them and we can't reverse it, promise me that you will not let me live like that."

Matt simply grunted. He wasn't having any of that talk.

Chapter 6

Level 1 protocol message

Dear Hanna.

Thank you for your reports, they have been most helpful.

Colonial I is fully refueled and its crew is now in stasis awaiting the Feb 2065 launch window to return to Earth.

Sorry to hear about your boy toy. I gather that he was a good man and could have gone places in the organization.

The problems with the hiberchambers have been noted and we will endeavor to have those fixed for the return flight. We can't have too many losses of assets in the future. You should be commended for keeping the first voyage casualties within tolerable limits.

I want you to continue your work in the lab on the Phase 2 study. I look forward to more progress reports. Dealing with this matter in situ is really the best-case scenario. It was good that you suggested that we complete this study on Mars.

It is time that you were made aware of previously classified information. As you know, Colonial I will not be back in Earth-orbit for a few years. We had always planned on dealing with the travel and launch window times by having multiple launch capabilities. There are two other ships that have been built. One is in geosynchronous orbit over China and the other is over Russia.

Colonial II and Colonial III are nearing completion and will make their launch windows next year in 2065. Colonial II has been outfitted as a colonial transport and will begin populating the second colonial site in the Alba Mons lava tubes. Colonial III is a mining transport ship and will immediately start transporting the raw materials extracted by the first colonial mining operations.

Your primary duty is to ensure that the mining operations are up and running in time to receive Colonial III. I have sent one of your brothers with Colonial II to oversee the operations on the second colony. I will arrange a visit for him to your colony once he is settled.

Hanna read and re-read the message. *This changes everything.*

Chapter 7

The group met in Hanna's room, all arriving at different times so as not to raise suspicion. Hanna brought them up to speed with the new developments from Central. For a minute or so, everyone was speechless.

Parm broke the silence. "I had always suspected as much. There is no way that the Company would put all of their eggs in one basket. Also, with the travel and launch window times, they would have to stagger the journeys or they would have been waiting twice as long to receive their shipments."

"Yeah," Matt added, "and this way if one of the ships is lost, there won't be an interruption in their plans. Built in redundancies. It's actually exactly what you'd expect from the Company."

"This, of course, means that our time table has moved up dramatically," Hanna explained further. "Whoever Hicks sent to the second site will be preoccupied with setting up, but at some point he will make the trip over to this colony to see how we have progressed, especially with the Phase 2 treatments. I have no idea who they've sent, but I can promise you that my brothers and sisters are all formidable opponents. They are also highly observant people. Anything out of order would immediately signal an alarm with the system."

"Why don't we just take him out before he arrives?" Carter asked. "If we could arrange for a little accident with the shuttle, we would take care of the problem."

"We're not gonna talk about killing people, are we?" Sandy demanded. "I thought we were all about helping to get people out of this nightmare?"

Jonas was equally appalled. "I agree with Sandy. I'm not about to start sanctioning terrorist activity. Isn't that what got us here in the first place?"

Hanna avoided eye contact with Jonas as she said, "As difficult as it may seem, Carter has a point. If we do nothing and my brother suspects anything, Central will not hesitate to take us down. If unsuccessful they could simply terminate all the colonists by turning the nanobots against them. That would include me. My hope is that this Phase 2 research will allow me to at least figure out how I was able to get my free will back. The problem is that if we then simply free the colonists, Central will just shut us down."

Parm looked down at his shoes and pinched between the bridge between his eyes. "So, we're back to getting control of Mars Local. As you all know, I have been working day and night on this problem since we arrived on this godforsaken rock. With help from Hanna, I have been able to determine that Mars Local seems to be the ultimate manifestation of the Company. While protecting the human population is important to the system, it is not the system's prime directive. The system's prime directive is maximizing profit for the Company."

Hanna went over to Parm and put a hand on his shoulder. She was starting to get the hang of moving around in the lower gravity. "You're doing great work, Parm, and we appreciate everything that you're doing. Are you getting any sleep? You look like you could use some. Why not come down to the lab and help me for a couple of days? Maybe you need to get your mind off the problem for a while and then come back to it?"

Parm sighed. "Yes, you're right. I am just going around and around in circles with this issue. I am sure that I can be of some assistance around the colony."

Matt stood up. "Okay, everyone. We know that we have a lot to do. Let's keep doing what we are doing and help Parm and Hanna in any way that we can."

With that, everyone got up. They timed their exits from Hanna's room to ensure that there was a definite randomness to it. Any kind of pattern might get them noticed.

Chapter 8

The team had agreed that eating together in the common dining hall would be a mistake. They took their meals with the groups that they had chosen to work with based on their skills. Matt, Sandy, and Carter were able to easily fit into the work crews given their mechanical experience. Parm was working with Hanna in the lab. Jonas was having the hardest time adapting; with the system directing the actions of all of the colonists, there was simply no need for management. Sure, the system had created a supervisor/worker structure amongst the workers, but this was just for efficiency and redundant oversight. Jonas was obsolete in this prefabricated society.

He couldn't get over how everyone interacted. The colonists weren't asleep; they were fully functional people who simply didn't control their own basic free will or emotions. They were always calm, always respectful. They were able to carry on what seemed to be normal conversations about the colony, their days, and even more strangely their previous lives. The system was able to put levels of influence on them when it served the system. At other times, this influence was relaxed, presumably to save computer-processing resources. It took every part of Jonas' being not to scream.

He was concentrating on staying calm and unemotional when suddenly one of the workers started acting unusually. He looked up and from across the room, Jonas could see a look of sheer terror in his eyes.

The worker started yelling, "Where am I! What the hell is going on?! Who are you people? You're all trying to kill me!" He flung his food tray violently across the room, standing to run across the floor. Within seconds he started to seize, and before Jonas could even react he dropped unceremoniously to the floor. The system had pulled his plug.

So, this is what it looks like to be shut off.

The workers simply turned back to their meals and started talking normally again.

Jonas could see Hanna instructing her nurses to remove the body, however the system had already sent two men with a stretcher to take the man away. Jonas had to concentrate hard not to react in any way. He couldn't give himself away now. He knew the rest of the team was doing the same.

He finished his meal and headed back to Hanna's room. She was so focused on her goals he hadn't seen her much at all. He felt like a fifth wheel in this entire thing. *Surely, I can be of some use to the team?*

Chapter 9

Hanna followed the two men with the dead worker. They were taking the body to be immediately incinerated. Hanna was in dialogue with Mars Local [via her implants]:

> *Requesting clearance to carry out autopsy on terminated colonist 437*
>
> *Colonist 437 terminated due to clearly aberrant behavior. Autopsy unnecessary.*
>
> *Autopsy to determine cause of aberration and avoid future terminations and loss of productivity.*
>
> *Calculating. Logic is sound. Proceed with autopsy.*

The two men carrying the stretcher suddenly stopped, and Hanna nearly crashed into them. They reversed direction, heading back towards the lab. Obviously, Mars Local had countermanded its original order.

Once there, she directed them to put the body into the automated medical scanner and surgical unit. This one unit was there to service the entire colony. She could just see the Company logic in failing to send doctors with the group. Where was the profit in that? She had surmised that the system had probably determined that the nanobots would deal with any minor medical afflictions, and that any serious accident could be handled by the single medical unit. A multiple injury catastrophe would presumably end with mass terminations; all very calculated. It made her sick.

Hanna cycled up the scanner and started the process of seeing what had gone wrong. Within a few minutes, she was able to see the worker's entire body system. Of particular importance to her was an analysis of the worker's endocrine, nervous, and cardiovascular systems. The nanobots had done an efficient job destroying the worker's heart and brain. It was brutal in its simplicity.

What Hanna needed to find out was how the worker had awakened. Had something gone wrong with the nanobots, or was it something else entirely? Some kind of innate characteristic that the worker had that was different from the rest of the colonists?

Hanna extracted some of the nanobots from the worker's brain. While she was working, she accessed the system to find out who this man had been. His name was Walter Jameson, a Displaced from Dallas. He had been transported here to work outside on the surface with the heavy mining machinery. Hanna reminded herself that he was a man, who had a family somewhere, who was now dead because the system had simply discarded him. She owed it to Walter to figure out how this happened so that he would not have died in vain.

Hanna had Rebecca and Jessie take the samples to the labs for analysis. The equipment being used for the Phase 2 work would be ideal to find out what had gone wrong with Walter. Or maybe, what had gone right.

Chapter 10

Parm and Hanna met in his small unit. The worker's accommodations were Spartan, making Hanna's simple room look luxurious. Parm had set up a working model for the system, off the grid, so that he was able to experiment with subroutines and viruses to attempt to penetrate the system. After three months, he had been able to create a virus that lived within a diagnostic program undetected.

"You see, the diagnostic program moves freely about the system without being noticed. As the *police force*, the system does not suspect a dirty cop. You can trigger the virus through your connection with Mars Local, allowing you to temporarily take over the system. How long it will last is a question that I can't answer right now. Also, I do not know what will happen once the virus is detected. Presumably, it will be wiped out, and then we're back at square one. Though the fact that there was a virus at all will probably create chaos back at Central."

"Good work, Parm. This could become very useful. At a minimum, it can act as a fail-safe if something goes wrong. Have you figured out how to introduce it without detection?"

Parm frowned. "That's the next problem." He turned back to his work desk and Hanna took that as a signal to depart.

Hanna was continually monitoring the progress of the colony through her implants; it worked like a beehive. It was quite amazing, actually, if you took away the human exploitation factor. Efficient and disciplined. Hanna imagined how effective a military force would be if under the same control, and her blood chilled. Of course. The only logical next step towards Company domination of the world, and the solar system for that matter, would be to have an army of soldiers with the same treatment. Earth Central could easily control troop movements with awesome efficacy. Loyalty to a country would cease to be an issue; the Company would simply control every soldier, from all countries. She could see the defense contract salesman promoting the benefits of nanobot technology in creating the ultimate soldier, who self-repaired and did not require medical attention. *I'm sure they also worked on musculoskeletal improvements that would be simply too enticing to any country. Every country.*

As her mind wandered, she could also see her brothers and sisters. There were over a hundred of them, inserted all over the world in key positions of influence. Government, military, business. The Company's master plan was undoubtedly in full motion. What could her small group do against that kind of machine? *Well, they must have an Achilles' heel. We just need to find it.*

Chapter 11

Sandy rolled off of Matt. They were both sweaty and thoroughly satisfied, breathing heavily. Sandy was just coming down from an intense orgasm. It was trust; she trusted Matt with her life. She trusted him in a way that allowed her to be herself. Her true self, not the tough Sandy who always pushed everyone away. She had never felt this way about anyone. *Is this what love feels like?* Sandy blushed and decided that getting all mushy might screw everything up.

"Well, we're getting pretty good at that," Sandy said with a little grin, her face all flushed.

Matt was getting his breath. "You're telling me. I wish we could just make love all day and forget about all this bullshit."

Sandy smacked Matt on the butt as he rolled out of the cot. They both laughed.

Matt's smile suddenly faded. "Just think, all these people. They might never feel the way that we just did. I bet their emotional dampening has a huge impact on, you know, intimacy."

Sandy said, "I have noticed that there haven't been any new pairings with the colonists. Even married couples don't sit together. They share quarters, but they sit with their co-workers. How will the colonists have children in the future?"

"I guess the system will just order people to bang when the system wants to increase the population of the colony. It's like cattle."

"Well, you're just a big buzz kill today, aren't you?"

"Yeah, sorry. I love you, Sandy. I really do. I didn't mean to bring you down."

That was the first time that Matt had ever said that. It made Sandy's heart skip a beat. *He feels the same way.*

Sandy was floating on a cloud all day - of course, only in her head. No point setting off system alarms now that she was in love.

Chapter 12

Jonas was working in the hydroponics section. Helping to sustain the colonists was probably the most worthwhile thing that he could do – that he had the skill to do, anyway. The clock was ticking on the depletion of the emergency supplies.

He actually liked the work. It felt like honest labor, something that he hadn't done a lot of in the past few years. There was no shortage of work in setting up the soilless system.

While Jonas worked, he had to marvel at the fact that the colony existed at all. The nuclear power plant drove everything. Without that basic energy source, the factories couldn't have produced the water, oxygen, hydrogen, methane, mineral extraction, and other basic needs for the colony. The mineral nutrients for the hydroponics crops were also extracted from the Martian soil.

Water, oxygen, nutrients, and light were the basic ingredients in building the hydroponics fields. It was quite the operation. Jonas had always envisioned one level of plants like he had seen so many times in pictures back on

Earth. In fact, this setup was horizontal and vertical like a warehouse, with stacked layers that went up at least fifteen feet in the air.

Jonas had to be very diligent to keep up with the other workers. They all worked with singular purpose and took very few breaks; only to relieve themselves and take sustenance on the fly. The nice thing was that they really didn't pay him too much attention, except when he got something wrong. Then he would get headshakes and would hear whispers. He would just shrug and carry on.

It was essential that the nutrient solutions constantly pumped through the trays would eventually hold the plant's roots. If the pumps broke down the plants would die very quickly. It was smart that the system didn't rely on one pump, but a series of pumps on different breakers, all of which had back-up batteries. The colony couldn't survive without the food that they produced.

Jonas had to smile as he wiped sweat from his brow. He had a purpose in this colony.

Chapter 13

Time passed quickly in the colony. There were hundreds of things to do to get the mining operation up and running. FLX Space Mining had landed all of the required heavy machinery and surface survival gear on the planet two years earlier. The raw material factories ran remotely and were fully automated, but the real mining work started when the colonists arrived. Surveying, testing, drilling, and other mining operations needed human bodies and minds on the ground. Colonists had been hand-picked for their mining skills, much of which had been earned working the Moon and Asteroid mining platforms.

Carter had placed himself on one of the surface work crews. His mechanical background allowed him to fit in easily, and he spoke the same language as many of the miners. He had no idea why the Company felt that they needed to control all of these people. He would have volunteered for this work and done it gladly. Perhaps it was power? Perhaps they had a need to dominate absolutely? There was no understanding the ruling class. *Those bastards just think they're better than all of us.*

Carter was outside when the first mining accident occurred. The Mars surface was very hostile, with a primarily carbon dioxide atmosphere, subject to dust storms and extremely low temperatures. In addition to this, any colonists working outside of the lava tubes had to be very careful about radiation levels. Surface shifts had to be short and efficient.

The dust storm started slowly and then exploded on the team, with hurricane level winds. Even though Mars Local had sent out a warning to the miners immediately upon detection of the storm, it came up so quickly it would have been impossible to avoid. Carter was in a transport vehicle with nineteen other colonists. He double-checked his survival suit to make sure that it was secured and airtight. The vehicle was fighting extreme winds trying to return to the colony, which was safely protected by the lava tube. Without warning, the vehicle flipped. Carter found himself hanging upside down from his shoulder harness, the driver's voice echoing out of the general intercom in his helmet.

"Please remain calm. An assessment of our survival is being made at this time."

That's comforting.

Of course, Martian dust storms had been the subject of study by Earth scientists for many years. The mining operation had been built with that knowledge, and the equipment that was delivered to the surface by FLX was incredibly robust, built to withstand even the worst storm. The problem was that this was not theoretical, it was real – and Carter was stuck in the middle of it.

The other colonists simply awaited further instructions. Carter decided not to wait around, and released his harness. With the lower gravity the fall wasn't as harsh as it might have been on Earth. He could hear the massive winds through the vehicle walls. There was no way that he could survive outside. Things were looking grim.

Carter activated his eyephone. The team had decided to stay off the cracked communication system except for emergencies. This certainly counted. His call was to Hanna, and she picked up right away.

"Carter, what's your status?"

"We flipped the truck! There are twenty of us trapped out here."

"Mars Local is calculating probable survival numbers. These storms can last for weeks. I'm concerned that the system may just cut its loses and terminate the trapped colonists."

"Nice."

"Parm has uploaded the virus program into my internal system. He found a way to get me in through the diagnostic programs. I'm worried about using it because it may tip them off, but if I don't, the system may just act without a second thought."

"You do what you have to do. I'll be fine for now, but all these miners are at risk."

"Okay. Sit tight. It looks like the other vehicles will make it back fine, it's just your vehicle that flipped. I'll call you if there are any further developments."

Carter couldn't do anything but wait.

Chapter 14

Hanna made her way to Parm's unit. He was there as usual, working on his complex technical and logistics projects. She was impressed with his dedication to their predicament.

"How goes the battle?"

Parm looked up from his workstation and sighed. "One step forward and two steps backward these days. The Mars Local security system is very advanced; I'm sure that the virus upload will work, but I have no idea how the system will react."

"Well, we may have use it sooner rather than later. Carter is trapped on the surface with twenty miners, and Mars Local is examining the storm. The data is still coming in, but if the system determines that this storm will last a long time, it may just terminate the miners. It may see the probability of a rescue being successful to be too small to bother with. Miners will die, and Carter would be trapped out there."

"And if Carter is eventually rescued, or if God forbid his remains are discovered, it will become obvious that he did not die at the same time as the other colonists," Parm said. "That might increase the security protocols and expose the team. We have been able to hide in plain sight by simply blending in. If the system puts a real eye on us, we will be noticed."

"So, we may need to act for a number of reasons. I will implement the virus now." Without further consideration, Hanna initiated a return to quarters message to the other team members. She then initiated the virus program. Nothing happened at first, as the virus had to be naturally carried with the diagnostic programs. Hanna may have been in a hurry, but the system was not; it simply chugged along at its normal pace. After a few minutes, the virus detected that it was in proximity of the Mars Local operating system. Hanna dipped her toe in lightly to see if there was a reaction. She tried to simply dim the overall colony lighting by half a percent for one second. Imperceptible to everyone except Hanna, who was able to perceive the dip in illumination. Then she waited. No negative reaction.

Hanna decided to be a bit bolder, and used the back door virus to access the Mars Local's emergency response system. The system was busy calculating the survival probabilities with data that was pouring in from surface and satellite sensors. The result came in that the storm would probably last for at least three weeks, and that a successful rescue mission of the flipped vehicle in the present conditions was below thirty percent. Hanna blocked this conclusion from being transmitted to the colony nanobot regulation system and then activated the emergency response team, who immediately mounted a rescue mission. She then retreated, allowing the virus program to become benign again, traveling silently through the diagnostic system. All of this happened in less than one second, but Hanna's implants allowed her to process data at superhuman rates.

The true test would be what happened next. Would Mars Local interpret Hanna's actions as an attack? Would security alarms go off? Hanna realized that she was holding her breath, and let it out with a big puff. Parm looked up at her with a quizzical expression on his face.

"Rescue team's off, and termination notice wasn't sent. I'm waiting for a response from Mars Local. Nothing yet."

"Thank God. That's what I had hoped, but I wasn't sure. The virus really is designed for little jabs and not a full-out assault. My hope was that its actions would work below the security radar. Mars Local should just interpret your activity as a higher-level override and move on. Moving forward we can probably use the virus to nudge when we need to."

Within a few hours, the overturned vehicle had been righted and was able to return under its own steam. The winds were howling and the rescue vehicles had moved slowly, but they persevered and all of the colonists were rescued. Of course, there was no fanfare. No emotion. The workers just returned and went to the dining hall for a long overdue meal. Carter had a hard time containing himself, but managed to do so for the sake of the team.

As it turned out, the storm lasted for over four weeks. The colony just rode it out, Mars Local reallocating the miners to other temporary colony activities. There was never any shortage of work.

Chapter 15

Rebecca was pregnant. She made the announcement in a matter-of-fact way one day when they were working in the lab.

"I have tested myself and I am now about four weeks along," Rebecca said, and then went back to the microscope and continued to analyze the nanobots that were destined for her child. There was no concern or worry about the dangers to the fetus.

"Who was the father?" Hanna asked.

"Is that relevant? I just went up to a bunch of different men while I was ovulating and asked them to inseminate me, and they did."

"We will have to do a paternity test at some point, for our research. It may become relevant in our Phase 2 research."

"Oh, sorry. I'll flash you their names and colony number designations right away."

As Rebecca forwarded the information, Jessica came in with some samples for analysis.

"How have you faired with your pregnancy, Jessica?" Hanna asked.

"I had sex seven times during my last cycle, but it doesn't seem to have stuck. I'll try different partners next time, hopefully I'll be more successful."

Hanna nodded her approval to Jessica, but inside she felt guilt well up inside her. She had to tell herself again that this was vital to their survival. She had to figure out how she had been freed from the grip of the nanobots and Central Command's influence.

Hanna did the math in her head. October 12, 2064 was Rebecca's due date. The colony was very much tied to Earth's calendar, even though it had nothing to do with the cycles on Mars. Mars' orbit of the Sun was six hundred and eight-seven days, however Central Command and Mars Local were synchronized to Earth time in order to coordinate launches and arrivals.

Hanna got back to her work. The male colonist who was terminated due to the supposed nanobot malfunction was presenting a problem. There was absolutely nothing that she could find wrong with the nanobots they extracted from Walter's brain. The only conclusion was that something had changed his brain chemistry so that the nanobots governing it became ineffective. Hanna had searched through his medical history and found nothing out of the ordinary. He had been prescribed anti-depressants after 911-2, but then so had most of the survivors who had eventually become the Displaced. There had been some behavioral issues and fights in his work record, but nothing that wasn't in most files. New Dallas was a rough place.

He had been twenty-five years old when he had died. That made him around sixteen at the time of the terrorist attacks. On a hunch she brought up the brain scans from the autopsy. She asked the computer to analyze Walter's against a normal brain to see if there were any abnormalities. What came up was alarming, but also fascinating. *Oh, Parm is going to want to hear about this.*

Chapter 16

Matt was in the middle of his daily exercise routine when his eyephone pinged. Breathing heavily on the combo step and upper body machine, he tapped his temple. Parm's image came on as administrator of the call, but it was clearly a conference call to the entire team.

"What's up, Parm?" Matt said, echoed by everyone else.

"We need a meeting as soon as possible in Hanna's room. Is everyone okay to meet? "

"I'm scheduled to leave for work up top in three hours, Parm," said Carter. "Will I have time?"

"Yes, you should be good to go," Parm said. Everyone else said that they could find a way to get out of their duties. Parm continued, "Stagger arrivals on the delta pattern on my mark. And mark." That meant that they would meet in approximately one hour, and everyone had their allotted times of arrival.

Once everyone arrived at Hanna's unit they got down to business. Even though there was a serious reason for the meeting, Matt was pleased to see everyone. The team had been so busy over the past number of weeks, helping to build the colony, they hadn't had a chance to get together as a group.

"I've made a startling discovery," Hanna said, skipping the small talk. "Walter, the colonist who died, was in the beginning stages of schizophrenia. While this disease usually sets in during a person's late teens, it commonly occurs in men up to twenty-five years old. He was twenty-four during the journey. It is possible that the treatment set the disease off, or perhaps it would have happened anyway. The bottom line is that the disease affects the structural connectivity of the brain. There was nothing wrong with the nanobots, it was a change in Walter's brain chemistry that rendered them ineffective."

"Well that's great, but we can't give all of the colonists schizophrenia, can we?" Sandy asked.

"No, of course not," Hanna said. "What it showed was that changes to brain connectivity are the key to thwarting the nanobots. Parm and I did some research on pregnancy. It seems that when a mother gives birth, oxytocin is released into the mother's bloodstream. This in turn triggers connective changes in the brain that have been said to account for the maternal instinct. This primitive and powerful brain function kicked in when I gave birth, rendering the nanobots controlling my emotions useless."

Parm elaborated. "So, theoretically, we may be able to figure out a way to synthesize a hormonal treatment for the colonists."

"But what about the men? That will only work with the women, won't it? Men don't have a maternal instinct," Jonas said.

Hanna shook her head. "While brain hard-wiring and connectivity within the male and female brains aren't the same, the actual differences between their brains are really quite small. Men also release oxytocin. They just do so under different circumstances, such as when they're in love."

Carter jumped in. "So let's assume that we can free all the colonists. Then what? As soon as Mars Local gets any whiff of anyone being free, it'll just terminate everyone with nanobots in their system."

Parm nodded. "Absolutely true, Carter. That is why we have to make sure that Hanna can shut down any kill commands before they happen. We've already had a successful test with the dust storm accident. We are confident that we can use the same virus to stop Mars Local from shutting anyone down."

Matt had been listening very carefully, and now he frowned. "That's a lot of ifs, guys. We have to be really careful moving forward to make sure that everything isn't lost. We're standing at a precipice right now. If we can free all of the colonists, then we have to be ready for the consequences. Even if we can get control of Mars Local and put the colonists back in control, you know that the Company will send everything that they have against us."

Sandy continued Matt's thought. "Logically, the Company will just send a nuke along with one of the Colonial ships and wipe us out."

"That's why we have to hit them first. The next launch window is in 2063. If we wait until the two vessels arrive, we could pirate them and use them to launch an attack on the Company space operations," Hanna said.

Carter shook his head violently. "That's insane!! They'll just launch missiles at us and blow us up on the way back to Earth! We'd be sitting ducks."

Parm was nodding. "And that, my friends, leads us to the final solution." Everyone turned to Parm as he began his explanation of the long-term plan.

Part V The Displaced

The Displaced were a disparate group of people linked together by the common experience of 911-2. The attacks on Seattle, Dallas, and Toronto had changed the world forever. It had changed the survivors into a group united in despair. The Mars colonization gave hope where there had been none. Had the Displaced who volunteered known what was in store for them, perhaps they would have chosen despair. - **Cassandra Taylor, chief colonial historian**

Chapter 1

Rebecca went into labor on September 24th, 2064. Hanna decided that the best course of action was to handle the birth herself, and had dismissed Jessica. Rebecca was very calm, her emotion and pain being controlled by the nanobots within her. Hanna had given Rebecca's child the in utero Phase 2 treatment a month before. She had truly wished that she hadn't needed to do that, but they could not deviate from the plan. In some ways, Hanna was happy that Jessica had been unsuccessful at carrying a child. Jessica had gone through two miscarriages before Hanna had ordered her to stop trying. She was convinced that they would get all of the data that they needed from Rebecca's childbirth.

As the labor progressed, Hanna monitored Rebecca closely. She had placed the other woman onto the medical surgical-and-scan table, and had enabled its scanning functions. She was going to make sure that she captured every part of the birth, and the effect that it had on Rebecca's brain.

As Rebecca became fully dilated, a strange look came across her face. She seemed to be panicked and unsure of her surroundings. Hanna knew exactly what was going on and flipped on very loud sample analysis device that she had strategically placed near the maternity bed.

"Rebecca, Rebecca... listen to me," Hanna said in a quiet but commanding voice near Rebecca's ear. "You are fighting nanobots in your system. The chemical changes in your brain are bringing you back to us. Just go with it. Know that I understand exactly what you're going through."

Rebecca looked startled and scared, but she was also going into a contraction and everything else seemed to suddenly become unimportant.

"That's right Rebecca, push now. You are nearly there."

Rebecca cried out and gave a final push. The baby arrived, and Hanna clipped the umbilical chord. Then she went through the normal newborn screening procedure and announced that Rebecca had given birth to the first Mars colony female child at 2:31 pm, Earth GMT. Hanna then talked Rebecca through delivering the afterbirth. In the back of her mind, Hanna knew that she was going to have to test the child for the success of the nanobot treatment, but for now everything checked out, so that could wait.

Hanna swaddled the baby and handed her to Rebecca. She stood beside the new mother patiently. Rebecca freed up one hand and slapped Hanna hard across her face.

"That's for giving my baby the nanobot treatments. There will be another one for making me sleep with those men. How dare you."

Hanna smiled while she reached up to her face. Rebecca was clearly back, and feisty at that. "Rebecca. We're all in danger at the moment, so it's critical that you remain very calm. I'm sure that the system is allowing certain increased behavioral peaks due to childbirth, but I'm not sure it will tolerate any further outbursts. Now that you're free of the nanobots, you have to be very careful. There are only a very small number of us who are free. Jessica is not. You cannot act in a way that will alert any of the other colonists that we are not subject to the control of Mars Local."

Rebecca went very quiet, obviously processing all of this new information. The baby started to stir and cry. Rebecca tried to encourage the baby girl to nurse, but after some time she was having a hard time and getting frustrated. Hanna, very grateful that her medical training at the academy had involved a rotation through the maternity ward, explained that Rebecca was producing colostrum and the newborn would really benefit from that. She helped Rebecca get her daughter positioned correctly and watched as her mouth went right over Rebecca's nipple.

"You'll get it, Rebecca. It takes patience and practice." Rebecca was looking down at her daughter and smiled. Then gave Hanna such a look of hate that it burrowed into Hanna's brain like a laser. Hanna realized with shame that she would have to live with her decisions for a very long time. She turned back to her instruments and started to analyze the results of Rebecca's transformation.

Chapter 2

Hanna and Jonas were in their quarters. Jonas was in a blind fury.

"How could you! After what you had been through yourself. Putting another woman through the trauma of forced pregnancy and the treatment of her unborn son."

Hanna hung her head. She had decided that she had to tell the team, and she owed it to Jonas to tell him first. She knew that he wouldn't understand.

"I know, Jonas. What I have done is inexcusable, but it's my burden to bear. I did this for the rest of the colonists. I could see no other way of determining what had freed me from the nanobot control. There was no other way."

"There is always another way," and with that Jonas stormed out of their room.

Chapter 3

Matt wasn't sure if Parm's plan would work, but none of the team could think of a better course of action. He was really happy that Rebecca had been freed – she would be a great asset to the team. Matt chuckled to himself. *The way Carter's doting on Rebecca and the kid, you'd think he was the father. I think he's smitten for Rebecca. We'll see where that goes.*

The day that Hanna had told them that Colonial II and III had both left Earth-orbit was a relief. The Mars launch window was now closed for another two years, and there was nothing that Central could do in the short-run to change the course of those missions. Their worst fear had been that they would be discovered before the launch, and that the ships coming would be nothing more than military ships bent on the destruction of their colony.

As far as the team was aware, Colonial II was delivering a thousand new colonists for the second site. Colonial III was delivering mining equipment, machinery, and colonial supplementary supplies. *I hope that includes a nice bottle of scotch.* Of course, Colonial I would remain in Mars orbit until the next launch window in 2065.

Chapter 4

Grant Foster was sitting at his console running through endless streams of data from the Mars colony. Grant was low on the totem pole, and he knew it. He had the inglorious job of going through low priority system functions to ensure that all systems were operating properly. It was a deadly boring job, and he counted the days to his next holiday break. They were months and months behind, but all of this analysis was third redundancy checking. There was never anything of consequence.

Grant was working on the Mars sandstorm and its effect on the colony. His super had wanted to get some recommendations from the analysis team as to how they might avoid future problems and how they could better deal with emergency response. Of course, Grant was only working in a tiny part of this project: how the system had reacted.

During the sandstorm, the system had gone into a cost-benefit analysis in regard to whether there should be a rescue attempt. Grant was reviewing the analysis and was puzzled by what he saw. It seemed that the system had actually come to the conclusion that a rescue was not likely and had recommended termination. Somehow, that recommendation had been overruled. Grant's first thought was that someone at Central had done it, seeing that there were miners trapped. The more he dug, though, the more confused he got. Central had not countermanded the request; it had come from the Mars colony. *But that's impossible.*

Grant called over to his supervisor, "Sir, you had better see this."

Chapter 5

Hanna was concentrating hard on one last, methodical check of her synthetic cure for the nanobot control when she became aware that Mars Local had raised the security level. She immediately launched the pre-agreed scramble alert through the team's secure eyephone network. *I hope that they get to their rooms in time to avoid detection.*

Mars Local was in the process of scanning all colonists and doing a full security sweep. Nothing was initially detected. Hanna held her breath, hoping that her people were safely out of the public and work areas. She looked over at Rebecca, who had gone to get her daughter from a crib that they had set up in the lab. Rebecca looked up with fear in her eyes. Hanna was sure that she looked exactly the same to Rebecca.

Chapter 6

Gregory Hicks had arrived at Central Command moments before the security sweep commenced. He had been alerted as to the anomaly in the system during the dust storm crisis and was determined to get to the bottom of it. They had far too much at stake to have any glitches in the system, especially among the worker drones.

The communications presently had a five-minute delay, quite short due to the proximity of Mars to Earth. The first visual images and facial recognition analyses started to come in shortly after his arrival. All colonists were accounted for through the nanobot net. Facial recognition was simply confirming that conclusion.

Hicks had his techs put all of the camera views up on the massive holoscreen in the command center. His enhancements allowed him to view and analyze many of the pictures at once, and he ordered the system to make every colonist stop and face a camera.

Hicks was impatient, as the order took five minutes to get through and then he had to wait another five minutes for the new images to start coming back. It was infuriating for a man who expected everything to be instantaneous. He was fuming.

The images came in. All of the colonists were standing very still and looking at cameras all over the colony. Not one of them was moving. Then Gregory saw a very small movement in the hydroponic farms.

"There, zero in on the hydroponics farm, now!"

The tech brought that screen up and Hicks had him focus on one area and magnify.

"Look, there's someone hiding there. Order the farm workers to seize that person at once and hold his face up to the camera."

Another ten minutes passed, and Hicks was about to explode with anger. When the images changed, he saw a man being held by two strong workers, and surrounded by all of the others. There had obviously been a struggle, and the workers had not been kind to this man.

The system analyzed the face. Within seconds the name of the man came up:

Jonas Harris.

But that's impossible! Harris is dead!

Chapter 7

Hanna was beside herself as she witnessed what was happening in real time through her mental-visual surveillance system. She saw the scanning happen, and then without warning she felt the order to grab Jonas in the farming area. At that point, she knew that she was also compromised, and the order for her termination was undoubtedly imminent. Hanna knew that with a single word, Jonas would be killed by the farm worker mob. She had to act, now; but if she did, she risked everything.

She made a decision, reaching out with her mind. The diagnostic programs were now saturated with Parm's virus, and she connected to every one. She activated all of them at once and ordered Mars Local to cut off all communications with Central Command. Then she ordered Mars Local to have the colonists release Jonas.

As before, nothing happened at first. Then she felt a shift. Mars Local did exactly what she said. She was in control of the local system – the viruses had worked. The question was, would they hold, or would they been seen as attacking the system and be wiped out? She didn't have time to find out.

They had to institute Parm's plan right away; there was no time. Hanna got Parm on the eyephone. He was as pale as Hanna had ever seen him.

"Parm, we've been discovered and we need to act. I've taken over Mars Local. I'm not sure how long it will last, but we have to act now."

"Agreed. I will alert the team to scramble."

With that Parm added the other members of the team and issued an Alpha One scramble. They all responded with the affirmative.

Jonas was on the move, having been released by the colonists. He was making his way to the medical unit, and to Hanna. The rest of the team started to move.

Chapter 8

Matt and Sandy had their marching orders. They made for the shuttle bay and quickly got into their flight gear. Matt had grabbed the extra-vehicular tools that they would need, and made sure that a functional spacesuit was on board.

Sandy jumped into the flight seat and started the launch sequence. The shuttle had been left by Colonial I, the other two safely stowed on the orbiting ship. Within five minutes they were ready to launch. The hypersonic vehicle was specially designed for the Mars atmosphere, and was a work of art.

Just before launch Matt jumped into the navigator seat. "I double-checked everything. We're go to launch."

Sandy was all business. "Roger that. Go to launch." *Can I really do this?*

Over the past few months Sandy had trained as a shuttle pilot in the shuttle simulator. Many of the other colonists were also being trained, so this wasn't seen as an anomaly by the system; but it was one thing to train in a simulator and an entirely different thing to be doing it for real. Sandy taxied out onto the Martian surface. *Those maintenance robots must have a full time job keeping this runway clear of dust.* Sandy chuckled.

"What's so funny?"

"Nothing, lover, buckle up. It's going to be a rough ride."

Matt crossed himself and smiled back at Sandy. "We have to get to the supply ship and disable the long-range communications array. If they get control of Mars Local again, we're sunk."

"Yes indeedy do…" Sandy hit the launch sequence and headed down the runway towards their mission in orbit. *No room for error, girl.*

Chapter 9

Jonas had made it to the medical center, where Rebecca attended to his wounds. Hanna was shocked at how beaten-up he was. The colonists had morphed into murderous animals with a simple command. She once again imagined what kind of soldiers Hicks was creating back on Earth. It sent a chill up her spine.

Jonas was breathing hard, but managed to get out, "Looks like Matt and Sandy are off. Have you heard from Carter and Parm?"

"Yes, Parm is coordinating the mission from his unit. I've ordered all the colonists into the common room, and Carter is locking down the exits. Hopefully, if there are any issues, at least all of the colonists will be contained."

"No kidding. I'm still trying to get over how they just turned on me. It was the scariest thing I've ever experienced. It was like they were acting as one, with absolutely no conscience. They all had a crazy look in their eyes. Like Mars Local was activating some deep-seated aggressions in these people."

Rebecca piped in, "Well, Hanna and I are really close to a cure. We've isolated the hormones that were responsible for stimulating my hypothalamus, amygdala, parietal lobe, and prefrontal cortex during labor, that caused my return to the living. We've synthesized them, and we can start trials. If we can change everyone back into normal people, then we can stop what happened to you from ever happening again."

"That's fantastic news, but if Matt and Sandy fail, Central could still activate kill codes and wipe all of the colonists out," Jonas said.

"So true, they have to knock out the long-range communications. Given time, Earth will surely figure out a security workaround," Hanna agreed.

Rebecca had a thought. "Has anyone ever considered what will happen when Mars Local's cut off and you lose control, Hanna? How will it act autonomously?"

"I've thought a lot about that," Hanna said. "Mars Local is really an artificial intelligence. Intelligence with no personality and no soul. The system will continue to act within the prime protocols set by its original programming. That means it will act to maximize profit for the Company as its prime directive."

Jonas groaned, but then added, "Well, one crisis at a time, folks. How's Carter doing with those exits?"

Hanna looked down at Jonas and felt intense guilt for having caused him so much distress at their last time together. "Carter should be reporting back soon, you need to rest. Just let us handle it." She put a hand softly on Jonas' shoulder and looked into his eyes. At first his face seemed bitter, but then his look softened. Tears welled up in Hanna's eyes. *Perhaps, he'll forgive me after all.*

Chapter 10

Gregory Hicks was calculating probabilities. Jonas was alive, which meant that Hanna was obviously aware of that. Therefore, Hanna had somehow gone rogue. If that was the case, then the colony itself might be compromised. He had seen complete compliance with the colonists, so the control systems were obviously working. Hanna had to be operating autonomously. She and her lover were up to something, but he didn't know what.

Hicks asked his team of experts, "Options?"

"Carry out a full systems diagnostic check of Mars Local."

"Eliminate Jonas and anyone associated with him immediately."

"We may have to consider that the colony has been compromised. A complete wipe might be necessary. Colonial II is on route and can re-populate the first colony and load Colonial II."

"Jonas may simply be on his own and hiding out for some reason."

Hicks had already considered all of these scenarios. He started pacing. There was so much at stake. He had a feeling that this was far more concerning that was immediately apparent.

"Terminate Hanna Smith immediately. Order the colonists to terminate Jonas Harris with prejudice. Further, order the colonists to carry out a search of the entire facility for any other unauthorized people."

"Yes, sir." The command order was sent and Hicks waited impatiently for the result. About two minutes after the order was sent, an alarm started to sound.

"Sir, we've lost contact with Mars Local. The order will not get through at this time. Running diagnostics."

Gregory Hicks slammed his fist down on the console. *Hanna, you bitch, what have you done.*

Chapter 11

Matt was tethered to the shuttle and was making his way to the communications array. Parm had walked him through this scenario a hundred times, but he had almost no experience with zero g and was finding the adjustment difficult. The suit was bulky and awkward, and his breathing was shallow. His heart rate was through the roof.

Sandy was speaking to him through his helmet communicator, but her voice sounded tinny and distant. "You need to take deeper breaths, Matt. You're going to hyperventilate. Close your eyes and get control for a second."

Closing his eyes, Matt focused on his breathing. *I can do this. I can do this.* Slowly, his heart rate went down and his breathing became more regular. *Focus on the task, jackass.*

Matt used his suit's thrusters to maneuver slowly over to the transceiver module. He was carrying a heavy-duty space tool-set designed to work in zero g. Once he made it to the array, he had to disable it. Parm had been very specific about this task. The digital transceiver was very robust and had a back-up system that would kick in if the primary system went down for any reason. That meant disabling both systems. The designers had taken into account normal wear-and-tear and other possibilities, but not outright sabotage. The system was optical instead of radio, using beams of light to send data packs to Earth. Matt had to cut through the thick protective cable-housing to expose the connective wiring, then he had to cut the wiring that allowed the ship to communicate with the laser housing. Once completed, he had to repeat the whole process with the back-up laser.

Matt found the process to be far harder than he originally anticipated. His hands were bulky in the thick gloves, and the tool was difficult to maneuver. It seemed that this simple task would take some time.

"How are you doing, Matt?" came the message over Matt's headset. He was concentrating so hard the sound startled him, but he appreciated the interruption.

"I'm working on the laser housing right now. If I can just get these damned tools to work, I should be done soon."

Matt went back to work. He managed to saw through the cable-housing of the first laser, then moved over to the second laser and repeated the processes. He had to fumble with the tools to get the proper clippers to complete his next task. Unable to pull the wires outs, he changed the tool to needle nose pliers. He then pulled the wires out through the housing, and had to replace the tool with the clippers again. *Kind of like building a BBQ back at home, I should have read the manufacturers manual.* Finally, he cut through the wires and was done. The communications to Earth were severed.

Matt let out a huge breath. He looked around him. The first time down to the planet, he had been in a box. This time he wasn't going to go back without taking a good look at his new home.

From this geosynchronous orbit, Matt could see the rust colored surface pocked with massive craters and old volcanoes. It was amazing to think that he was floating above this dead planet; the place where he would probably live out his life and die. *You really are a morbid bastard.* Matt made his way back to the shuttle and the love of his life. *Well, everything isn't all bad.*

Chapter 12

Parm was tired. No, he was exhausted deep in his bones. He felt the entire weight of the responsibility for this colony on his shoulders. Matt had been successful and Hanna's control of Mars Local was holding. Carter had contained the colonists.

Parm had been working in this little unit for months and months, theorizing, designing, planning. He had used every ounce of his intellect and knowledge to get his friends through this seemingly impossible situation. At no time had he thought that they had anything but a slim chance of success, but that did not deter him. His heritage told him that freedom from tyranny in any form was the most important of human rights. His people had lived under the thumb of a foreign colonial power headed by a corporation for hundreds of years. *I cannot let that happen to my new people.*

Parm stood up and his back cracked. He was stiff all over from hours of sitting, his neck and shoulders sore. He felt many years his age. He stretched and made his way to the lab. He needed the walk anyway. Maybe Hanna would have some news on the cure for the colonists.

As Parm walked down the hall he had something nagging at the back of his mind. He couldn't put this finger on it. *Probably nothing.*

Just before he was about to key in the entry code for the lab, he stopped short.

Colonial I. Parm turned around and rushed back to his room.

Chapter 13

"This had better be good," the Captain said, talking to herself. The ship system had awoken her from hibernation and there was a video message waiting for her. She viewed it at her personal quarters communications console.

The Captain clicked on the video. Gregory Hicks' image came up on her holoscreeen.

"Captain Johnson. Please be advised that the Mars colony is now under the control of a hostile force. Hanna Smith has shut down communications between Central Command and Mars Local. We are unable to see or hear what is going down on the surface. Central Command needs control of Colonial I's communications system immediately. We also require that you send a team to the surface to assess potential losses to the mining operation."

The Captain replied immediately, "Sir, communications are at your disposal, however my crew is not trained in military operations, nor are they being paid to carry out reconnaissance missions of the kind that you are contemplating." The Captain awaited the reply. Five minutes there and five minutes back. *Time for a coffee.*

Chapter 14

Gregory Hicks received the video reply from Captain Johnson. *We should have used the nanobots on the ship's crew.* There had been a feeling among the logistics team on Earth that captains and navigators needed to have complete flexibility of thought and action in order to respond to emergency situations; system control might result in a crucial microsecond delay in decision making. In space, it was ninety-nine point nine percent boredom and point one percent sheer terror. His analysts had said the flight crew needed that edge, but now they might present a problem. At least they had communications, and his team was working on a workaround. The Colonial I ship system acted as a nanobot interface during the voyage from Earth. There had to be a way to re-activate command over the colonists.

Chapter 15

Along with her other professional training, Hanna was trained as a scientist. She was not happy with the level of certainty over the potential efficacy or safety of the nanobot cure, but they couldn't wait any longer. Carter had let one of the colonists exit the common room, and Hanna had ordered her to the lab through the nanobot network.

The young woman was on the surgical and scanning table. They were going to monitor the progress of this treatment very carefully. Hanna's hands were shaking when she prepared the injection that contained the synthetic cure. Rebecca nodded her head and Hanna injected the woman.

The young woman lay very still. Hanna was instructing the system to keep the woman calm and unafraid. Suddenly, the woman started to scream and trash. Hanna and Rebecca had to use all of their strength to keep her down before she passed out.

"Is she dying?" Rebecca asked in fear.

Hanna was reviewing the data as the scan surveyed the young woman's body. "No, the dosage must have been too much. I was afraid of that. The stimulation simply overwhelmed her."

Hanna and Rebecca waited for ten full and slow minutes. The seconds ticked by like an eternity. Then, the woman's eyes fluttered and opened.

"Where am I? What's going on? Oh my God." The woman had a look in her eyes, like a deer in the headlights of a car.

"What's your name, sweetie?" Rebecca asked.

"Joan. My name is Joan. I went under on the ship and now I'm here, but I have all of these strange memories. I was working in the colony farms. We attacked that man…" Joan suddenly sat up. "That man, we attacked him. I kicked him. Is he alright?"

Jonas, who had witnessed all of this from his recovery bed, spoke up. "I'm just fine, Joan. Welcome back to the real world."

Joan twisted around and looked at Jonas. She let out a sigh and closed her eyes.

"Lie back honey, you've come through a lot and need to rest," Hanna said.

"Thanks, thanks so much," Joan said, falling back on the pillow.

Rebecca looked directly at Hanna. "It worked. It really worked."

Hanna just nodded her head, thinking about dosages and possible side effects. She wasn't willing to accept victory just yet. "Let's try this with one of the men." Hanna was counting on there being more similarities than differences between male and female brains.

As she was being to prepare the next shot, Parm's identification came up on her eyephone.

Chapter 16

Parm contacted Matt and Sandy on the shuttle and looped Hanna in. "Good work Matt and Sandy, but we have another problem."

Matt closed his eyes and opened them. "What's up, Parm?"

"I just realized that Colonial I is a potential problem. I'm assuming that Central Command will take over the ship communications. There is a smaller, but quite capable nanobot control system on board. They might be able to work around the Mars Local system and cause all kinds of problems for us."

Hanna was shocked. "Of course. How could we have missed that?"

Parm shook his head. "This is my fault. I was so focused on Mars Local, it never occurred to me that they might have a contingency plan."

"There's no time for blame right now. What should we do?" Sandy asked.

Parm suggested, "Stay in orbit for the time being and await further instructions. We may have to get you to repeat the procedure with the Colonial I communications system. The problem is that their crew could simply repair it, so any advantage would be short lived."

Hanna said, "I will contact Colonial I and have a chat with the captain. She's tough, but I never got the impression that she was heartless. I just hope that she wasn't subjected to the nanobot treatment."

They logged off and Hanna immediately dialed up Colonial I. Captain Johnson came up, with some serious bed head, coffee in hand.

"Captain Johnson, I'm sorry to have to be contacting you under these circumstances."

"From what I hear, you've staged some kind of coup down there."

"As with every story, there are two sides. I would very much appreciate if you would listen to what I have to say before you pass judgment on us."

Hanna went on to take the Captain through the entire story, from the faulty hiberchambers, to her awakening, to the enslavement of the colonists through the nanobot therapy. She went on to explain how her small group had figured out a way to neutralize Mars Local and to cure the colonists of the nanobot control. When Hanna was finished, the Captain paused and then cocked her head.

"Well… that is probably the most incredible story I have ever heard. You actually expect me to believe all of that?"

Hanna had been ready for that reaction. "Please upload the attached data packet. This includes evidence supporting everything that I'm saying, including the scientific specs for the various therapies and cures. The package also includes video footage of Central Command's physical control of the colonists through the nanobot system. Also, I'm a senior executive of FLX Mining, and have intimate knowledge as to the internal workings of the corporation, including information at the highest clearance level.

"If you allow Central Command to reinstitute control of the colonists, they may well institute a kill command, terminating the entire colony. They will certainly do so for me, as I am subject to the physical nanobots in my system. Further, you would be allowing a corporation to continue the exploitation and control of a thousand innocent citizens of Earth."

"Well, if you put it that way, I'll have to contemplate what you're saying. Please give me time to review your data pack. In the meantime, I will agree to block any communications between the ship and the planet. Captain Johnson, out."

Hanna contacted Matt and Sandy. "We're going to need you to maneuver into close proximity to Colonial I. Please stand by. We may need you to board and secure the ship, or to disable the communications system."

Sandy replied, "Roger. Will bring shuttle within range of Colonial I." Matt began looking around the shuttle for possible weapons.

Chapter 17

Captain Johnson received the second video from Earth. As promised she allowed all Earth/Mars transmissions to the ship, but set up an override of the ship-to-Mars transmissions.

The Captain poured herself another coffee and opened the data packet from Hanna. The video images were startling and disturbing. She saw the colonists all stand as one and face the cameras. She saw the attack on Jonas in the hydroponics farm. She reviewed the scientific data, but it meant little to her. The question was, could this be true? Had FLX Mining actually gone so far as to enslave the colonists? Was she a slave trader? The Captain had an image of the old colonial vessels traveling from Africa to the New World with slaves in their hold. How did those captains feel? It was legal; it was commerce; it was fundamentally wrong.

Captain Johnson was going to have no part of it. But what could she do? There would be no returning to Earth if she sided with Hanna. The Captain remembered something that her father had told her once. "The only thing necessary for the triumph of evil is for good men to do nothing." Berg or Burke, she couldn't remember. Well, sexist as the statement was, the Captain felt that it rung true.

She opened the video feed from Earth. Hicks came on the screen.

"You are hereby ordered, under the emergency Company charter that you signed on with, to get control of the situation on the planet. Awaken your crew and head down to the planet immediately. There is a weapons hold that is now available to you. The location and combination for those weapons are now at your disposal. Central Control will be implementing a system reboot shortly. Please carry out these orders immediately."

The Captain sighed and grabbed her coffee mug. Keying in the code to the massive cargo hold, she made her way to the secret weapons cache.

These guns may come in handy in the days to come.

Chapter 18

The Captain came up on Hanna's holoscreen.

"You can get your people to stand down. There's no need for your shuttle to board Colonial I. I hereby relinquish control of this vessel to the Mars colony."

Hanna sighed with relief. There was only one more thing to do. After a moment, she looked up and addressed the Captain. "Thank you for your wisdom, Captain Johnson. You are most welcome to join us at the colony, as are your crew. I would imagine that it might be more comfortable here than in an Earth prison."

"Thank you, Hanna. I will have to revive the crew. Unfortunately, I can't risk them staying in hibernation, as Central Command may figure out a way to override my command authority and put one of them in command. I cannot guarantee that they would all make the same decision that I made."

"I understand, Captain. I have recorded a message for Earth. Can you please broadcast that on an open channel, and include the new data package that is attached?"

"What is it?"

"The truth."

"Do you think the Earth wants the truth?"

"Well, they may not want it, but they need it. I'm concerned that what's going on here may be going on back on Earth as well."

"I hadn't considered that. Well, send away. I'll wake up the crew and join you on the planet. Would you mind having the shuttle dock? I may need some help convincing the crew to come peacefully."

"Will do."

Captain Johnson had the weapons set out on the flight deck navigation table. There was enough firepower to take out a small army. *But I don't think a small army is coming.*

The Captain set up a continual loop for Hanna's video feed. *I guess this is my answer to your order, Mr. Hicks.* The broadcast went out by both digital and analogue transmission to Earth:

Citizens of Earth.

My name is Hanna Smith. I was until recently a senior executive with FLX Space Mining, a subsidiary of FLX Energy. I was sent with Colonial I to setup and operate the first mining colony on Mars for FLX Space Mining.

I am sending this message on behalf of the Displaced, the new citizens of Mars. We declare Mars to be a sovereign nation, protected under the provisions of Article 1 (2) of the Charter of the United Nations, declaring equal rights and self-determination of peoples.

The citizens of Mars have thrown off the shackles of slavery perpetrated upon them by the Company, a cartel of multi-national corporations who presently control the majority of all corporate interests on Earth. Individuals such as Gregory Hicks are in control of this cartel. We hereby claim all FLX Energy, Worldstar, and FLX Space Mining property presently on or in orbit around Mars as partial reparations for the atrocities committed against our citizens.

Mars workers were controlled by technologies manipulated by a central computer system.

Evidence of this violation of basic human rights is attached as a data packet. Please be warned that it is our sincere belief that this technology is presently being used by the Company on Earth.

Mars will welcome any of the Displaced currently living on Earth. This offer includes the colonists presently on route via Colonial II. If any Displaced can get to Mars, there will always be a home for you here.

Mars will trade with Earth and welcome all friendly vessels, however any aggressive action will be considered an act of war.

On behalf of the sovereign nation of Mars we wish peace and prosperity to all of the citizens of Earth.

Epilogue

John McDonald woke in his hiberchamber in Colonial II. Immediately, he started to receive data from Central Command. Within seconds he had uploaded the entire Mars situation, and was processing scenarios and probabilities for taking the colony back for the Company. *My sister, I am coming.*

www.ingramcontent.com/pod-product-compliance
Lightning Source LLC
Chambersburg PA
CBHW060518180626
46817CB00002B/402